Steiner Farm

T. James Peters

Copyright © 2020 by Timothy Peters

All rights reserved. No part of this publication may be reproduced, distributed, or transmitted in any form or by any means without the prior written permission of the author.

ISBN 9781708878009

I.

Like most teenage boys not yet old enough to drive, the Beck brothers liked to wander around town engaging in minor mischief. It was their first time in the St. Hubertus cemetery though. They climbed monuments, hopped gravestones, and looked for anything interesting that may have been left by mourners.

Before Cole knew anything was wrong, his brother Boone had disappeared, and Cole found himself in the shadow of a large looming man in a black dress. The man was clean-shaven, and his thick hair glistened like chrome on that sunny day. Cole felt deep trepidation.

"Why are you here?" the man asked.

"I live just outside of town," said Cole.

"I meant why are you here, in my cemetery?"

"We were just playing. We didn't steal anything."

"A cemetery is holy ground, not a playground."

"I'm sorry, we didn't mean any harm."

The man's tone softened a bit. "Do you go to church son?"

"No sir."

"Well then, you should come to mass here on Sunday." Cole looked skeptical, so the man added, "We have donuts after mass."

Cole perked up at the mention of donuts. Seizing the opportunity, the man pushed forward with his impromptu evangelization. "Do you see that field of Christmas trees over there?"

"Yes sir."

"On the other side of the field is my cabin. You're welcome to go there and help yourself to a Coke if you want, but you can't stay here in the graveyard."

At this, the man and the boy parted ways. The boy, heedless of the risk in accepting this type of invitation from a stranger, set off for the cabin. The man headed to the rectory.

The boy followed the gravel road, passing through an open gate with a sign overhead that read "Steiner Farm." The farm, once four hundred acres, was now three hundred and sixty. After inheriting the farm in 1917, Gerhard Steiner, who was the first of that name, tithed forty acres for building a church, school, parish hall, rectory, convent, and cemetery. For the next seventy-five years, the parish of St. Hubertus and the Steiner family became intertwined. These days, that bond was stronger than ever. Msgr. Augustine Steiner, who the boy had just met, pastored the parish. The school principal, Sister Paul Joseph, who had been born Mary Steiner, was Msgr.'s sister, and three of their sisters, Magdalena, Clara, and Margaret worked at the school, sharing duties in the office and cafeteria. Sometimes with good natured humor and other times with derision, parishioners and outsiders referred to St. Hubertus as, "the Steiner family business."

A girl in the porch rocking chair saw Cole coming and called out "Who are you?" when Cole was in hearing distance.

Not expecting the cabin to be occupied, Cole responded nervously, "Uh… The man in the black dress said I could come here and get a Coke." To Cole, the girl seemed about his age, but maybe a little younger. She was skinny and pale, and her looks didn't make much of an impression on him.

"First of all, that's not who you are and second, it's a cassock, not a dress."

"What?" He was completely flummoxed by this strange girl.

"I asked who you are, and you told me who sent you and why."

"Oh, I'm Cole."

"Do you expect me to believe Uncle Gus would send someone to his cabin that didn't know any more about him than what he was wearing?"

"Never mind, I'm leaving."

The girl stood up and lured him back. "Don't be so sensitive. Come on and get your Coke."

The cabin was tiny and lacked modern conveniences. "Do you live here?" he asked the girl.

"It depends what you mean by 'here.'" Cole rolled his eyes. He wasn't used to having this level of precision in conversation.

She relented. "I don't live in this cabin, but I do live on this farm. We have a trailer down the road."

With that, the boy and the girl ran out of things to say to each other, so they drank their Cokes in silence. When they finished, the boy, teasing the girl, thanked her for her hospitality and began to leave. The girl stopped him though. "I'm here a lot."

"What do you mean by here?" he managed not to sneer.

The girl nodded in approval of the boy's quick wit in using her words against her. "I meant this cabin," she said. "I come here a lot whenever my mom's in love." The boy did not understand the connection, so the girl explained, "My mom falls in love a lot. She'll get a new boyfriend and he'll be at our place all the time. They immediately start saying things like 'we this' and 'our that' like they're a family. I can't stand to be around it, so I come here, and they hardly notice I'm gone."

"Oh." Cole understood that.

"Believe me, it doesn't usually last long. They'll get in a fight and it's back to 'I this' and

'My that' until she falls in love again." The boy had no response, but was enamored of the girl. She was clever and sassy, but did not hesitate to show him her vulnerability. He decided that he wanted to be part of her life.

Like many children in the 1980s and 90s, Cole Beck and his brother Boone were raised by a single mother, but they were even more feral than most in their generation. Their mother worked part-time at a local gas station in addition to her full-time job as a nurse's assistant. Two jobs and the symptoms of what would ultimately be diagnosed as Lou Gehrig's disease left her with very little energy for parenting.

Their mother and father had never married. He drove trucks cross country, and had used to visit the boys and their mother when he passed nearby. Their mother would provide a hot meal, a warm bed, and tepid affections, while he provided nothing but a periodic reminder she had missed her chance to be married. These visits became fewer and farther between and then stopped altogether. Relieved, the boys and their mother figured that he had found other stops to make, but they never discussed him out loud. They didn't want to jinx it.

So, when Cole left the girl, like most evenings, he returned to a parentless home. Not even looking away from his television show and bowl of cereal, Boone asked how much trouble he got from the preacher. "It was bad," Cole said, "The man threatened to call the cops and shoot us if we came around there again."

Boone chuckled with no remorse for leaving his younger brother to take all the responsibility for their actions. Cole did not care though. He was still thinking of the girl.

II.

Cole had passed by St. Hubertus church almost every day of his life, but he had never paid much attention to it. The church was not big, and its steeple was not tall, and it was camouflaged by the Ozark rock masonry typical of the area's roadside buildings. Cole expected the inside to be equally nondescript, but when he stepped into the bustling church building the next Sunday morning, Cole was awestruck by the church's beauty. The stained glass windows glowed, and the ceiling was painted with an angel-filled sky. And in the front, a large and intricately carved wooden structure cradled a shiny gold box. Cole considered it the fanciest place he had ever been.

Cole went to church that first Sunday for the donuts, but he returned each week thereafter when he discovered the girl, whose name was Jen, attended weekly with her aunts and grandmother. Short visits after mass slowly turned into planned meetings at the cabin. They drank Cokes and meandered around the Christmas trees, talking about teenage things. They were confidants, but not romantically involved. With the way that the girl spoke of her mother's antics with men, Cole sensed that she was not interested in dating.

Nevertheless, Cole did things to impress Jen. His largest overture was joining the church.

At the Easter vigil in 1994, fifteen-year old Cole Beck received the Catholic sacraments of initiation. Msgr. Steiner was like a proud father at the vigil mass. He had come to know Cole very well, having ushered him through the conversion process, which was called RCIA by the Church. Msgr. Steiner appreciated the Lord's hand in converting the heathen cemetery loiterer, and turned a blind eye to the boy's true motivation.

Soon after and at the invitation of Msgr. Steiner, Cole began serving mass on Sundays as an altar boy, and eventually daily at 7:00 am. Msgr. Steiner began to utilize him as a tradesman would an apprentice. Cole accompanied Msgr. to hospitals and funeral parlors, and to the homes of parishioners. The calls were sacramental, business, and social, or usually, some combination thereof. Msgr. also ensured that Cole had money, paying him for odd jobs around the parish grounds. Msgr. Steiner guided Cole as a true father, and Cole loved Msgr. as he would have his own father, had his father been there for him.

Their most frequent social call was to visit Msgr.'s mother, Wilhelmina. She lived at the house on Steiner Farm, along with her three daughters, Magdalena, Clara, and Margaret. The three Steiner sisters worked at the school, and collectively, Wilhelmina called them the spinsters. She had no qualms illuminating their failure to marry and have families of their own, since she was convinced, "there was nothing wrong with them other than they were too scared to do it."

    The Big House, as it was called, wasn't even that big, just bigger than the one room cabin that sat just down the road on the farm. In the early years of their marriage, Wilhelmina and her now deceased husband, Gerhard II, lived in that cabin along with the first three of their thirteen children. Before the birth of their fourth, Gerhard built the three-bedroom, two-story, and one-bathroom Big House. The parents had a bedroom on the first floor, and upstairs there were two bedrooms, one for boys and one for girls. During their first couple years in the Big House, the separation by gender was equitable with two boys, Gerhard III and Augustine in one bedroom, and two girls, Mary and Katherine, in the other. The division wasn't fair for long, as the Steiners ended up with three boys and ten girls. But even now, Wilhelmina insisted on having a room for boys and a room for girls, so the spinsters shared a room, while the other stood empty.

    At eighty-two years old, Wilhelmina was still independent and insisted on cooking for Msgr. Steiner whenever he could get away from his pastoral duties and, "wasn't too busy playing with his Christmas trees." During his first visit to the Big House with Msgr. Steiner, Cole introduced himself to Wilhelmina with his best politeness.

"It's a pleasure to meet you, Mrs. Steiner," he said after telling her his name.

"You can call me Grandma. Now, I know I'm not your grandmother, but to me, it's an earned title like Captain or Doctor, not a relationship." When Wilhelmina was a little girl, her family called her Minnie, a moniker derived from her first name. As an adult though, she never achieved five feet in height, so her nickname changed to Mini. She had tolerated the nickname because her husband liked it, but after he died, she made it known to all, family, friends, and neighbors, that she was to be called Grandma.

Now, after meeting her grandmother, Cole realized that Jen came by her sass and wit naturally, and smiled before responding. "Then, it's a pleasure to meet you, Grandma."

Soon after, Sister Paul Joseph entered the house with a bucket of wild blackberries. Whether Sister was teaching school, attending mass, or picking blackberries, she was always dressed the same, in a knee length skirt and sweater vest; only the length of the sleeves under the vest varied by season. As always, Grandma Steiner greeted Sister Paul Joseph using her birth name. "Hello Mary, will you stay for supper?" While Grandma Steiner appreciated that her daughter answered the call to religious life, she never understood her name change, often asking, "Why couldn't she be Sister Mary Steiner?"

Hurrying to the kitchen with the bucket, and ignoring her brother and the young man, Sister Paul Joseph responded, "No, I have a meeting at school."

As Sister Paul Joseph returned from the kitchen, Grandma asked, "Cole, have you met my granddaughter, Jen?"

Before Cole could reply, Sister Paul Joseph answered her mother in a soft tone, but with condescension. "Mother, you've seen them together after mass."

Grandma concurred, "Oh, yes, of course, maybe we even talked about it. You know sometimes I forget things." Sister Paul Joseph glared at Msgr. Steiner, but he refused her eye contact as their mother continued, "Jen's smart and strong. Very German, maybe a little too German, being stubborn as a mule at times. She has a foul mouth too, but overall she's a good girl despite her mother's efforts, and will be a good wife to the right man."

Msgr. then interrupted, "Cole, will you please go to the cabin and bring us a couple of Cokes?"

Cole responded dutifully, and when he returned, Sister Paul Joseph had already left. Grandma, Cole, and the spinsters took seats at the table, and Msgr. stood over the table and blessed the food. The six then feasted on German pot roast, mashed potatoes, and green beans. For dessert, Grandma served peach cobbler with black coffee. Cole tried to tell her he was not a coffee drinker, but Grandma scoffed, "Nonsense," and handed him the cup anyway.

After dinner, the spinsters washed dishes, and Msgr. Steiner watched the St. Louis Cardinals game in a recliner while Grandma led Cole around the house explaining the important pictures and mementoes. Two particular items were most dear to Grandma and held prominence of place. The first was self-explanatory, but Grandma proudly told the story anyway, showing no emotion. It was a triangular wood box housing a tightly folded American flag. A brass plate on the box read, "PFC Gerhard Steiner 1932-1951." To Cole, the second item looked like a framed handkerchief, and he couldn't even make a guess when Grandma asked, "Do you know what that is?"

At Cole's blank look, Grandma explained, "At a priest's first mass, he presents that to his mother. It's the cloth he used to wipe the blessed chrism from his hands at his ordination. It's called a manutergium. When I die, I'll be buried with it to present at the last judgment and say, 'my son, too, shared in your Priesthood.' At that mass, the priest also gives to his father the stole that he wore for his first confession. My husband was buried with Augustine's stole."

Msgr. rarely heard his given name and only from his mother, so it snatched his attention from the baseball game. He checked his watch, "We'd better head on down the road, morning's bearing down on us already."

Cole thanked Grandma for the meal and she responded, "I hope you come again, maybe Jen will join us."

Oblivious to Grandma's matchmaking, Cole responded, "That would be great."

III.

Cole's favorite social calls were to Eldringhoff Farm because of the food. Frederick Eldringhoff had a renowned vegetable garden and orchard, and according to Msgr. Steiner, his wife, Annette, was "the finest cook in the history of St. Hubertus not named Wilhelmina Steiner." Msgr. mentioned the Eldringhoffs in each of his wedding homilies, not because he had any idea what went on behind closed doors at their house, but as an illustration of how marriage partners should complement one another. Msgr. would explain, "From his labor, Frederick provides premium ingredients that Annette, through her skills, transforms into culinary delights." The example made perfect sense to parishioners, but was lost on any visiting wedding guests.

Cole did notice an odd formality that Msgr. had with Annette. He almost always referred to parishioners by their first names, but he called Annette Mrs. Eldringhoff. So, during their short drive home from Eldringhoff Farm one evening, Cole asked Msgr., "Why do you call her Mrs. Eldringhoff?"

Msgr. smiled as though he knew a secret and said, "Oh, we're old friends." The response made no sense to Cole, so Msgr. clarified. "It's because we're old friends." Cole still didn't see the connection, so Msgr. explained, "It's hard to pastor a parish of strangers, but it's even harder to pastor loved ones. You see, one of the sheep became the shepherd, so I have a lot of shared history with my flock. I can't change the past, but I can take measures to remove any doubt about my current motives or loyalties. It's imperative for any priest to maintain his virtue, even before his ordination. But for me, the pastor of family and lifelong friends, there cannot be even a whiff of impropriety."

IV.

One rainy autumn evening during Cole's junior year of high school, Msgr. told him that they needed to make a quick stop on their way home from a wake. They pulled up to a small wood house that was in disrepair, and Cole recognized Sister Paul Joseph's car parked in front. Msgr. took an envelope from the glove box and told Cole, "Wait here, I'll be right back." He left the truck running and the wipers on low, then jogged to the porch with impressive speed for a man of his age. He waited there for a moment until the door opened. A teenage girl came out to greet him and Cole recognized her from school. Msgr. entered the house and the door closed.

The girl was Kristen Ambuehl. She was a year ahead of him in school, and her sister Amanda, was a year behind him, in Jen's class. He also knew that they had an even younger sister, who was not yet in high school. The girls' mom had died from cancer over the summer, and with their father in prison, Kristen, who was eighteen, was now the guardian of her two younger sisters.

Msgr. Steiner returned to the truck after a couple minutes and said, "Sorry, but I thought it best if you weren't involved in this one."

As Msgr. pulled onto the road, Cole asked, "The Ambuehl girls live here?" Msgr.

nodded. "I didn't know they were parishioners. I've never seen them at church."

"They're not. Their mom went to school at St. Hubertus, but fell away from the Church as a teenager. She reached out to Sister Paul Joseph near the end, scared for her daughters." Msgr. glanced at Cole, then returned his eyes to road. "Priests don't just prepare souls to go to heaven, we pick up the broken pieces left behind on earth." Msgr. was a stoic man, but seemed bothered talking about the woman and her daughters. He cleared his throat and said, "She was able to go to her rest, knowing her daughters would be cared for."

V.

Notwithstanding his apprenticeship to the priest, Cole remained focused on Jen. He wanted to be her boyfriend, but she never opened the door, even a little, for anything other than the relationship they already had. Nothing he tried changed her posture, so when he was seventeen years old, he decided to force the conversation.

Boone had managed to have his driver's license revoked by the age of nineteen. He sometimes drove anyway, but he usually imposed on someone else for a free ride. It was not odd for him to get a ride somewhere without having a way home and then hang around, stranded, until Cole came to retrieve him. This time it was Jefferson City. Cole invited Jen to come along, thinking that the thirty minutes in the car alone with each other would be a great opportunity to broach the subject of evolving their relationship. Thinking he may need the full thirty minutes to make his pitch, Cole jumped right in after she shut the car door.

"Um…, In the three or so years that we have known each other, you have been my best friend."

Confused Jen replied, "Correct."

"I want you to know how important you are to me."

"Thanks," said Jen. "You are important to me too."

Cole stumbled on, "But I also want our relationship to be more."

Jen replied quickly, "More what?"

"More official."

Wary, Jen asked, "What are you doing?"

"Trying to be your boyfriend."

"No." Jen was closed now.

"Don't you want more from our relationship?"

"No, dammit. And you should shut up while we're still friends."

"But why, Jen?"

"This is not going to happen." Jen stared stone faced out the front window.

"But why not?"

"Because I don't need that. I need you to be my friend."

"Why can't we be both?"

"Because that's not what happens." She finally turned to look at him, imploring, "Look, you're in love with me and I could be in love with you, but for how long?"

"Maybe forever."

"No, we'll be in love until were not." She turned back to the front to stare out the window. "And then you'll leave me."

"You don't know that's how it will end."

"Cole, shut up and drive the car or let me out." Cole shut up and drove.

VI.

Msgr. Steiner hoped that Cole would go to seminary, but he had applied no pressure, never even asking the boy if he believed the Lord was calling him to the priesthood. Parishioners, however, began to ask, and with increasing frequency. Cole had never committed either way, avoiding a direct answer. Now though, Cole was nearing high school graduation, and like most fathers, Msgr. Steiner considered it time to talk to the boy about his future.

Msgr. Steiner recognized that Cole's options were limited. His mother had stopped working due to the progression of her disease and could not even support herself with the disability payments. She'd finally had to move to a nursing home. Cole and Boone cobbled together enough money each month to stay in the small house that their mother had rented for as long as they could remember, but Cole knew that the arrangement was untenable. Msgr. Steiner knew it also, and asked Cole to the rectory one day after morning mass. They sat at the kitchen table and after his first sip of coffee, Msgr. asked, "Do you have work lined up after graduation?"

Cole replied without hesitation, "I was thinking about the Army."

Msgr. nodded, "That's not a bad plan, if that's what God is calling you to do."

"I feel like God is calling me to support myself, and that is all of the vocational discernment that I can afford."

"I see… And if you could afford vocational discernment?"

"Then I would go to seminary."

VII.

Jen objected at first when Cole informed her that he was moving to St. Louis for college. But after she thought about it, she came around and announced, "I'll move there too after I graduate. Even if I don't go to school, I'll just get a job. Then, we'll only have to be apart for one year." But when Cole told her that he would be going to seminary to become a priest, Jen became sullen and withdrew from him. Cole was perplexed by her reaction, but said nothing.

After this conversation, Cole and Jen remained friends, but their relationship was not the same. Cole tried to mend their friendship before leaving for college; he bought them tickets to the 311 concert in St. Louis. Cole had hoped to surprise Jen with the tickets in private, but Boone found them in the mail first and asked while Jen was at their house, "What are these for?"

"Jen and I are going." Jen was obsessed with 311 and forgot that she was mad at him, giving Cole a tight hug that lingered.

After seeing Jen's reaction, Boone said, "I'm going too."

Cole pushed back though, "You don't even have a ticket."

Boone answered, "I'll buy one there or just hang out in the parking lot."

Trying to head off a fight, Jen said, "Cole, it's fine."

Cole could have fought harder to exclude Boone, but he didn't want to tell Boone his real intentions for the trip. Cole expected that Boone would weaponize that information and use it against him. So, Cole caved and allowed Boone to ride along, but banished him to the back seat.

Not long into their trip, Boone's motivation for travelling to a concert without a ticket became clear when he opened his back pack and displayed a plastic baggie of joints and a bottle of Southern Comfort. Cole admonished Boone, "You won't be able to take that into the concert."

"I'm not going into the concert. I'm going to sell all this in the parking lot. Well, not all of it. The bottle is for us to share, and I have a joint for each of you, for letting me come along."

Cole could not remember Boone ever showing appreciation for anything and presumed some sinister explanation for the personality anomaly. Boone offered a joint to Cole, but he refused it. "No thanks, I'm driving."

Jen rolled her eyes, "Like you would anyway," and she and Boone laughed.

Jen and Boone shared the joint first and then the bottle. When they arrived at the concert, the bottle was only one-third consumed, but Jen was all the way drunk. Leaving Boone in the parking lot to conduct his business, Cole and Jen rushed to the amphitheater. Jen wanted to see the opening act, The Urge, and Cole wanted to get away from Boone.

During the concert, Jen acted like any drunk teenager, and Cole was irritated. Her face was pale from intoxicants and she was sweaty from dancing in the mugginess, with rogue strands of bleached hair stuck to her cheeks. When 311 played "Beautiful Disaster," Cole commented, "They named a song after you?"

Without hesitation, Jen snapped, "Cole, don't be a bitch." It was the first time that Cole ever felt dislike for Jen, but at the same time, he never wanted to love her more.

When they returned to the car, Boone was asleep in the back seat, but still holding the now empty bottle of Southern Comfort by the neck. Jen wanted to sleep as well, so she lifted the arm rest and used Cole's right thigh as a pillow. After a couple minutes, still resting her head in his lap she asked, "Are you mad at me?"

Cole looked in the rear-view mirror to ensure that Boone was sleeping before answering, "No."

"Okay, well, are you disappointed in me? You barely said anything to me all night." Cole thought about an answer, but Jen continued when it took him too long to reply. "It would be good for you to lower your expectations for me. I sometimes think that you hold me to a standard of what you want me to be and not what I am."

Cole whispered to not wake Boone, "I want you to be exactly who you are."

"If that was true, you wouldn't be disappointed in me."

Cole didn't respond, and Jen fell asleep. About thirty minutes later and without even opening her eyes, Jen asked, "Cole?"

"Yes?"

"I love you, but I won't be with a guy I can't afford to lose."

VIII.

Cole's mom passed before he left for college. She was irreligious and died a pauper, so she was cremated without fuss. The funeral home scheduled a memorial service, but only Msgr. Steiner, Jen, and an administrator from the nursing home attended. Boone wasn't there, and Cole received the attendees alone. When Boone returned home that night, Cole greeted him sarcastically, "Thanks for coming today."

Boone was unapologetic though. "I had to work. I don't have a sugar daddy like you."

Shocked by the insinuation, Cole answered defensively, "That's not what he is."

"Well from what I can tell, you're not doing anything with your little girlfriend. So, there must be a reason for that, right?"

Disgusted, Cole went to his room and closed the door. He sat on the edge of his bed and thought about his mother, and then his father for the first time in years. Cole's memories were interrupted by the sounds of Boone greeting a guest. He recognized the young woman's voice as one of Boone's regulars. Then, as expected, he heard Boone's bedroom door close.

IX.

Cole left for college a week after his mom's funeral. Msgr. Steiner paid Cole's tuition and sent him money every month for living expenses. Msgr. also arranged for Cole to work at a local Catholic school assisting with before and after school care. Cole was ambivalent about the kids, but liked that he was paid to play games and sports. He also did not mind the attention that he received from the single young ladies working alongside him at the school. One of Cole's coworkers, Mary Beth Hogan, went to college with him as well.

Like a model, Mary Beth was tall and graceful. Her green eyes were almost too big for her face and her hair was a shade that other blondes purchased. She was so pretty that most young men would not approach her, and the few that did lost interest after learning of her commitment to remain a virgin until marriage. Mary Beth didn't meet many young men who met her high standards for a potential husband, but when she did, she was proactive.

Mary Beth pursued Cole, even after he told her he wanted to become a priest. She flirted with him, baked him cookies, and agreed with everything he said. One day after the children had left, Cole helped Mary Beth carry the toys to the storage shed. While they were inside and concealed from their coworkers, Cole sensed that Mary Beth wouldn't mind it if he kissed her. So, he did, and he liked it.

Overnight, Cole thought about other options than the priesthood. Maybe he had a vocation to marriage after all. Even when he thought he still wanted to be one, he wondered whether as a priest, there would always be a Mary Beth, and he questioned whether he could say no for the rest of his life without ever saying yes. For the next week, he spent time with Mary Beth outside of work, mostly hanging out on campus. Then, Mary Beth invited Cole to have dinner with her family and Cole accepted.

Mary Beth's parents and six younger siblings lived on an estate on the outskirts of suburban St. Louis. Their house was massive and in the style of a European country manor. The interior walls were wood and adorned with tapestries and hunting trophies.

Mary Beth introduced Cole to her parents and he greeted them as Mr. and Mrs. Hogan. Her dad insisted, "Call me Jack," and her mom hugged Cole before saying, "I'm Theresa." Cole thought Theresa was just as pretty as Mary Beth and that they could easily be mistaken for sisters, and he said so. Their parish priest, Fr. O'Connell came to dinner as well and Cole could tell by the dynamic that Mary Beth's parents were important patrons of their parish.

After dinner, Jack invited Cole to a room in the basement he called the parlor. Cole did not know what a parlor was, but by the smile on Mary Beth's face, he assumed it was a good thing to be going there. The room had a fireplace, a bar, and two club chairs with a standing brass ash tray between them.

Jack poured brown liquor from a crystal decanter into two glasses cut in the same pattern. He handed one to Cole and set the other on the mantle, so he could make a fire. Cole then noticed the mantle. It was a large piece of walnut. Carved into the left corner was a heart wrapped in roses and pierced with a sword; into the right corner was a heart crowned with thorns; and in the middle, was the head of a stag with a crucifix between the antlers.

Cole said, "St. Hubertus."

Jack had no context for the utterance, and asked, "Who?"

Pointing to the deer carved into the mantle, Cole repeated, "St. Hubertus. That's his stag."

"I didn't know that. Fr. O'Connell introduced us to a woman who specializes in Catholic art. We went to her studio and when I saw this mantle, the deer just spoke to me."

"Spoke to you?"

"Not literally, but like art speaks."

Cole explained, "The deer did speak to Hubertus though."

"Really?"

"Yeah. St. Hubertus was a hunter who pursued a great stag on Good Friday instead of keeping the day solemn. Instead of fleeing, the stag stopped and faced him, displaying a crucifix between his antlers. Hubertus then heard a voice warning him to turn to the Lord and lead a holy life or go to hell."

"I guess I should be more careful about which days I hunt." Jack smiled, then said, "I presume Hubertus obeyed, based on the S and T in front of his name."

"The voice sent him to a local bishop for spiritual direction, and he eventually became a bishop himself."

With the fire crackling, Jack and Cole sat in the club chairs. Jack offered Cole a cigar, but he declined. After Jack lit his, he said, "She's coming after you pretty hard, isn't she?"

Cole was discomforted by the question, but responded with candor. "Yes, this has been a new experience for me."

Jack shook his head. "Her mother and I have encouraged her, for her own sake, to calm it down, and to be subtle, but all she has ever wanted was to get married and have a family. She's even told us we're paying for college so she can get an M.R.S. degree." Cole chuckled because she had told him the same thing. "She's my daughter and I know I'm biased, but I think it's special that a person her age knows exactly what God is calling her to do, and is trying so hard to do His will." Jack puffed on his cigar and leveled with Cole. "If this doesn't work out for you, I get it. I just pray that she won't be discouraged."

From his own experience with Jen, Cole understood Jack's concern too well and nodded in agreement.

Cole was even more drawn to Mary Beth after meeting her parents. He never had a normal family and would have liked to become part of theirs. Cole and Mary Beth went on more dates. They were all the same though. Mary Beth agreed with everything Cole said and wanted their future to be the way Cole wanted it. Then, at the end, they would kiss. For Cole, something was missing. So, he ended it gently, explaining, "I just don't think we're being called to the same vocation."

X.

Jen didn't know how long she had rested her head on the steering wheel before she forced herself out of the car. Now upright, she headed toward the doors of the abortion clinic. On her way, a woman stopped her and asked for just a moment of her time. Jen was in no hurry to do what she had come there to do, so she stopped. The woman whispered, "Are you sure you want to do this?"

"I'm here, aren't I?"

"That's not what I asked," The woman's voice was soft and kind.

"Of course I'm not sure, but I'm trying to get it over with, so I don't have to think about whether I'm sure anymore."

"I did that. I got it over with, and here I am, standing outside this God forsaken place almost a half century later, so you won't have to do the same." Jen fell silent, so the woman asked, "Where are you from?"

Unsure at first whether she wanted to share personal information with this stranger, Jen took a risk because the woman seemed sincere. "St. Hubertus."

"I'd ask whether you're from the town or the parish, but we both know they're one and the same."

"You know the place then?"

"I'm from there too, but I haven't been back since."

Jen understood what the woman meant by "since."

Then the woman asked, "Can I buy you lunch?"

Jen looked at the clinic and back at the woman, then said, "Okay."

Neither Jen nor the woman ate much at lunch, but they talked for almost two hours, and the woman shared her story. "I found out I was pregnant after my boyfriend left for the Korean War. When I found out he had been killed, I panicked. I just didn't think I could do it on my own. So, I went to a farmhouse near Eldon and a woman there ended my pregnancy."

Jen winced. She didn't ask for specifics, but imagined the procedure had been painful.

The woman then asked, "How about you?"

Jen took a deep breath, then admitted, "It's not that I can't do it."

"Is it that you don't want someone to know, like a parent or the baby's father."

"It's someone, but not either of them." Jen was struggling to verbalize the truth, and the woman gave her time to answer. "It's my best friend."

"Well, if she's a true friend, she won't shame you for this."

XI.

Cole did not return to St. Hubertus until the end of his first semester. He had heard very little from Boone, and had no desire to spend time with his bother anyway. When he visited for Christmas break, Msgr. Steiner stayed at his cabin, amongst his beloved Christmas trees, and let Cole have the rectory to himself. Cole was glad to stay so close to Jen, who still lived with her mother in the trailer on Steiner Farm. Cole and Jen had talked by phone, but their conversations were vapid, surface level exercises. Cole wanted their old relationship back and, after he dropped off his bags, headed to her place with the intention of fixing their friendship.

As soon as Cole entered the trailer, he sensed that something had changed about her. She looked different and carried herself more cautiously. He did not know what it meant until he saw the engagement ring on her finger and she said, "I'm pregnant."

Cole sat in catatonic silence, so Jen continued, "And I'm getting married."

Eventually Cole responded, "I see that."

"I'm sorry that I didn't tell you sooner, but I didn't want to over the phone."

Cole was slow to reply, but he insisted on truth from her, here in person. "You mean you didn't want to tell me at all."

"You're right, I didn't want you to know."

"Why not? It not like we're together, per your wishes."

"Cole, I'm marrying Boone. It's his baby."

Cole left the trailer without a word and returned to St. Louis that night. In the next week, Cole received letters from both Jen and Msgr. Steiner. In hers, Jen pleaded with Cole, "Please don't hate me. I was lonely without you, and I screwed up." Cole couldn't believe her audacity, blaming him for her predicament, and although he was alone in his apartment, said aloud, "You two deserve each other." The letter from Msgr. Steiner read simply, "My son, the Eucharist is all that matters. In Christ, Msgr." Cole tossed both letters in the trash.

After a couple miserable days, Cole reached out to Mary Beth to see if she was available for dinner. Mary Beth sounded glad to hear from him, but declined. "I'm sorry, but I have a date, and it's already pretty serious."

Cole respected that, and instead numbed his pain that night on a bar stool. He told his story to the bartender who was more than twice his age. She could tell his heart was shattered, so she said things, and later did things to him, that made him feel better, but only for that moment. He couldn't help but think of his tryst with her as his first mortal sin. Cole was crossing a line, and felt troubled. But every time thereafter was easier, until he did not even notice there was a line to cross at all.

Late in his freshman year, Cole spent the night in the women's dormitory with a girl he had just met. In the morning, he crossed paths with Mary Beth in the hallway. They didn't exchange words, but her disappointment was palpable. Cole was disgusted with himself, but not enough to change his behavior. He realized he had stopped thinking of the priesthood altogether, but unwilling to risk a disruption in his financial support, didn't tell Msgr. Steiner of his change in plans.

XII.

Jen's mom, Paula, the youngest of Grandma Steiner's thirteen children, had almost no reaction to learning that her teenage daughter was pregnant, as if it was an inevitability, or even an expectation. She believed Jen would be "better off" marrying the father, but encouraged her to "test it out" first. So, Boone moved into their trailer. Paula gave them the only bedroom in the trailer, but wasn't too inconvenienced since she spent most nights at her boyfriend's place.

Only several weeks before the birth of their son, Jen and Boone married in a civil ceremony attended only by Paula. Afterward, they celebrated with a meal at Frau's Haus, a local tavern serving homestyle food and the best place to eat without going all the way to Jefferson City. At Frau's, they discussed possible names for the baby.

Boone said, "The boy should be named after his daddy."

Paula agreed. "That's right, he should."

Jen, however, knew that the world did not need another Boone Beck and proposed a compromise. "What if we named him Bo?"

Boone nodded with approval, but still negotiated. "Only if the next one can be Hunter."

Nearly choking on her drink, Jen questioned Boone's sanity, "Next one?"

Soon after the baby's birth, Paula broke up with her boyfriend and moved back into the trailer. Bo was only six weeks old when Paula lost interest in being a full-time grandmother. She ceded the trailer to the young family and moved to Florida with a new boyfriend.

XIII.

When she found her sister had left town, Sister Paul Joseph visited her niece and the new baby in the trailer. She wanted to see if she could help in any way as Jen was young and inexperienced with babies.

Boone accused Sister Paul Joseph of, "meddling," though, and rejected her offer. "We're fine."

Sister Paul Joseph ignored him and looked to Jen for her answer. Jen didn't say anything, but nodded in agreement with her husband.

Sister Paul Joseph voiced her concerns to Msgr. Steiner when he arrived at the Big House for supper that evening. "I'm sick thinking about that poor girl and her baby stuck in the trailer with that cur."

Msgr. agreed, "He is worthless, but what do you suggest we do about it? Do you want me to have a talk with him?"

Sister Paul Joseph didn't think Boone was salvageable. "Your talk won't mean a thing to him. I'm thinking about throwing him off this farm. As the trustee, I decide who lives here."

But Grandma Steiner rebuked her daughter. "Mary, you'll do no such thing."

"Mother, she's too young for this."

"What's too young? She's the same age I was when I had Gerhard."

"But Boone is awful. He's no help."

Grandma scoffed, "You think your father was a helper? He was a pious man, but he had high expectations for a wife. No one came and rescued me when I struggled to keep up with kids and a house. I had to figure it out on my own, just like Jen has to."

Sister Paul Joseph wouldn't relent. "Do you really want that for her?"

Grandma Steiner held firm, "This is not even close to the worst thing that's happened in that trailer. Paula had strange men in and out of there, with her daughter as a witness! It was disgusting. Jen, on the other hand, though she got herself into a difficult situation, from what I can tell, is trying her best to be a good wife and mother. You know, when Paula came to me, pregnant with Jen, I knew that the only chance to raise her baby right was on this farm, so I let her put that trailer over there. And now again, Jen's best opportunity is on this farm and close to us."

Defeated, Sister Paul Joseph was silent, but Msgr. reiterated, "Like I said before, I can go talk to him."

Grandma quickly quashed that as well. "Absolutely not. You don't interfere between married people. They need to figure this out on their own."

Msgr. Steiner tried to pull religious rank on his mother. "As a priest, it's part of my job to do things like that for my flock."

Grandma pulled an even higher rank, "You may be my pastor, but I'm still your mother, and I said no."

XIV.

Jen stayed at home with the baby while Boone worked whatever out-of-town construction job he could get. For the most part, he was only home on weekends. Even though they were married, Jen had no access to Boone's money. He didn't have a bank account and only used cash. Before leaving for the week, he'd leave Jen money. It was usually enough, but barely.

When Bo was four months old, Jen told Boone, "I need more money this week." Jen was washing dishes at the time and mentioned it in passing while he rested on the couch.

"For what?"

"To buy clothes."

"You have clothes."

"Yeah, I have maternity clothes and all my old stuff in size four, but I don't see either fitting in the near future."

Boone got off the couch, walked to Jen at the sink, and put his arms around her from behind. Jen cringed and closed her eyes as though she was being fondled by a strange lecher, and not her husband. Boone either didn't notice or care about her reaction, and asked, "Would it be so bad if you were back in maternity clothes?"

Jen didn't answer. Instead, she turned to smile at Boone. She already knew how to get money from him. It was a chore for her because she didn't like him, much less love him, but it worked. Boone left town early the following morning, and when she woke up, Jen found a hundred dollars more than usual on the dresser.

XV.

Grandma Steiner's fifth child, Elizabeth, left home at eighteen years of age to pursue her academic interests. When she first proclaimed to her mother that she was a feminist, Grandma Steiner sassed, "Of course, women are superior to men, but I didn't have to go to college to figure it out. I learned it the old-fashioned way, by fixing supper only hours after giving birth and never having a day off sick." That exchange strained their relationship, with both mother and daughter feeling belittled for their chosen vocation. Thereafter, Elizabeth only returned to the farm when necessary.

Looking out her kitchen window, Jen saw Aunt Elizabeth walking down the gravel road from the Big House and wondered what in the world she could be doing there. She barely knew the woman, but Jen nonetheless welcomed her inside. Elizabeth declined Jen's offer of a seat and a drink and stood near the door, obviously uncomfortable.

"Are we alone?"

"Bo's sleeping in the back, but otherwise, yes." By the look of distaste and confusion that crossed her aunt's face, Jen could tell that Elizabeth had no idea whether Bo was the baby or the father. "The baby, Bo?" She could have found out the name of her husband and child before coming here, thought Jen.

"Yes, of course." Moving on, Elizabeth asked, "How are you?"

"I'm fine."

Looking around the trailer, Elizabeth pressed her, "Are you though?"

Jen was becoming impatient and let Elizabeth know it. "I said I'm fine, and I meant it."

"Jennifer, what is your plan?"

"To keep my son fed, clothed, and sheltered until he can take care of himself."

"That's a plan for your son, but what about a plan for you?" Sensing that Jen didn't have one, Elizabeth continued, "Bring your son and come live with me in Columbia. You're a smart girl. You can go to college and someday have a career, and give your son a better life. I can help you with that."

Usually stubborn, Jen actually listened to her aunt with an open mind and considered the offer. She wanted a better life for her son, but didn't know if that was here with his father or there with an educated and independent mother. "I'll need to talk to Boone first."

"What? Why? You have to leave that boy…"

Jen interrupted to correct her aunt. "You mean my husband?"

"…before it's too late."

Raising her voice, Jen responded, "Too late? I'm nineteen years old."

"If you stay here with him, how long will it be until you're saddled with another baby?"

Becoming defensive, Jen responded with surprising precision. "Thirty-four weeks."

Aghast, Elizabeth asked, "But why?"

"I'm doing what I have to do."

"Have to?" The look of concern on Elizabeth's face was unmistakable. "If you think that's what you have to do, then you're not actually fine here."

Growing even more agitated, Jen replied, "I said I'm fine, three times now."

Disgusted, Elizabeth rubbed her eyes while she thought about the situation. "Who knows about this?"

"No one else."

"Then, it's not too late to take care of it. Come with me today. Get your baby and let's go."

Jen was struck by her aunt's choice of words. To Jen now, taking care of a baby meant feeding, diapering, and bathing, and certainly not what Elizabeth was suggesting. "You've never had a baby, have you?" Jen asked Aunt Elizabeth, not unkindly.

Elizabeth stopped but didn't answer.

So, Jen settled the matter. "Thank you for your offer to have me and Bo live with you, but I'm not going with you, anywhere."

"You're going to stay here with him and two babies?" Elizabeth asked, "This is going to be your life?"

"No, maybe we'll have three or even four."

Elizabeth walked out without another word.

XVI.

With his graduation approaching in May of 2001, Cole knew what was coming when Msgr. Steiner asked to meet for lunch in St. Louis. Like the other times Msgr. had visited Cole, they ate at Salume, an Italian sandwich shop. Msgr. had developed a taste for mortadella during a trip he made to Rome as a young priest. Mortadella wasn't available in central Missouri though, so he never missed an opportunity to eat it while in St. Louis. Cole didn't share Msgr.'s opinion of mortadella, considering it just a fancier name for bologna, so he ordered a salami sandwich instead. While they waited for their sandwiches, Msgr. said, "The vocations office thinks that you are no longer interested in seminary."

"Oh…" Cole felt his heart thump.

"Since you stopped communicating with them."

Cole sighed, "I've been having a hard time, and I just don't think I can be a priest anymore."

"What do you mean by hard time, son?"

"My faith is gone."

"Because of my niece and your heathen brother?"

"It's not just that."

"What else then?"

Cole looked down at that table, "My lifestyle is…, let's just say it's unchaste."

"That's not the same as a loss of faith. That's a choice to not follow the rules. Have you lost your faith in God?"

"I don't know, but I've stopped living a Catholic life altogether. I cannot imagine becoming a priest at this point." Their order number was called, and Cole looked to the counter and back at Msgr., welcoming the distraction from the conversation. Msgr. nodded, and Cole went to get their food.

When Cole returned, Msgr. Steiner continued. "You're wrong if you think that I have some vested interest in you becoming a priest. I do, though, worry about your salvation. You have put your soul in jeopardy because my niece hurt your pride. That could be tragic for you, so it's important to me. I told you about my older brother Gerhard, right?"

"Yes, he died in the Korean war?"

"Well, he is the reason I became a priest. You see, Gerry was a great kid. A good student, athlete, son, and brother. Everyone loved him. Shortly after he left for the war, I heard rumors that his girlfriend may be pregnant. No one ever confirmed this, and she moved away before it became obvious one way or another. To this day, I don't know if it was Gerry's baby or if she was even pregnant at all. But none of that haunts me. What keeps me up at night is the possibility that my brother died a hero, but unrepentant of mortal sin, and is burning in hell. Maybe he didn't commit a mortal sin or if he did, maybe he was absolved before death. I don't know, but the possibility torments me to this day. I forwent having a wife and family and all the comforts that they provide so I could help young men like you and Gerry, good boys enjoying life, but lacking awareness of their own mortality. The devil's most effective trick is convincing people that they have plenty of time. It's too late for Gerry, but the good news for you is that you can still repent, do penance, and amend your life."

    Cole already knew that he could be absolved of his sins with a simple confession, but he also knew he was unwilling to change his life. Cole had not lost faith in God, but just the will to live faithfully. Msgr.'s story was persuasive though, and Cole chose to err on the side of caution. "I think I'm ready to make a confession."

    "Very well. Let's eat first." He picked up his sandwich and smiled at Cole, "You should pray though that you don't die in the meantime."

    Cole had confessed many times before, but never in the cab of Msgr.'s truck, and never with such a robust list of sins. Afterward, Cole felt the fatherly love that Msgr. Steiner had for him, welcoming him back with open arms. Cole was ashamed that he had taken advantage of Msgr. Steiner's generosity in paying for his college, and privately vowed to again discern in good faith whether he was being called to a priestly vocation.

XVII.

Our Lady of Providence Catholic School in suburban St. Louis dismissed early on September 11, 2001, and kindergarten teacher Mrs. Lillian Ward rushed home. She was unnerved by the terrorist attacks and wanted to be near her husband, Jimmy, and infant daughter, Gemma. Lillian and Jimmy had started dating in high school, after they partnered for a class project on the Free Exercise clause. Neither dated anyone else, before or after, and they married while still in college. Both were self-conscious teenagers, Lillian because she was a bit chubby and Jimmy because he was so small. As adults though, Lillian was a comely woman who had matured into her body, and likewise, Jimmy grew to be, if not tall, at least a regular sized man.

Their apartment was small, even for a one-bedroom, and Lillian panicked when she noticed that the baby was neither with Jimmy nor in the bassinet they had wedged between the couch and the wall where an end table once stood. "Where's Gemma?"

Keeping his eyes trained on the news coverage, Jimmy answered, "Sleeping on the floor in the bedroom."

"Why isn't she in her bassinet?"

"Because I wanted to listen to the news and thought she would sleep better in the other room."

"You couldn't have moved the bassinet to the bedroom?"

"She's fine. I put a blanket down."

Lillian was tempted to ask whether Jimmy would like to sleep on the floor, but restrained herself in the interest of marital harmony. She took a quick peak at the baby in the bedroom, then joined Jimmy on the couch, and rested her head on his shoulder.

With a flat affect, Jimmy mentioned, "I passed the bar."

Lillian sat up. That news deserved acknowledgement despite it being a solemn day. "Congratulations," she said, and smiled. When Jimmy didn't react, Lillian continued, "Are you going to take the job at my dad's firm?"

"Corporate law? I can't spend my career fighting the rich on behalf of the wealthy."

"Well then, what are you going to do?"

"I don't know."

"Well, please figure it out quickly. We need a bigger place to live and that can't happen on my salary alone."

"We don't need to move right away."

"You're right, we have about seven months."

"Why seven months?"

"Because I'm pregnant."

"Again?" He blurted. But then Jimmy's faced changed as if he already understood the gravity of his reaction.

But Lillian wasn't angry. Instead she was thoughtful and earnest.

"When you wanted to quit law school after two weeks, I encouraged you to give it at least a full semester. And you did, but your mind was unchanged that it wasn't what you wanted to do with your life. So, I said you had invested too much to simply walk away, and you stayed in school for me. You resent me for it now, but I didn't do it to control you, but to be a cheerleader for you, because I believed that you could do great things as an attorney. You've been so unhappy though, and I've blamed myself for that. So, I tolerated your brooding. And now, you are so morose that you cannot even fake an appropriate response to learning that we are going to have a baby."

Jimmy offered neither explanation nor apology. Instead he said, "I'll call your dad about the job."

But this didn't make Lillian happy, the way he thought it would. "Jimmy, I already have a Catholic mother. I don't need another martyr in my life. Just go find a job that won't make you resent me."

XVIII.

With a clean conscience and a new will, Cole started seminary in the fall of 2001, and he excelled. His apprenticeship with Msgr. Steiner gave him a clear advantage over his peers. Cole also relished the fellowship he had with his classmates, and he developed a brotherlike bond with his roommate, Enzo Cucci.

Although seminarians, Cole and Enzo were still young men with natural inclinations. So, on Fridays nights, they caroused, and not in low-key pubs, but high-octane dance clubs. Cole wasn't a dancer, but he would because it was the safest way for him to experience the satisfaction of a woman's attention. Each night before going out, Cole and Enzo would always agree to leave the club together and without companions.

One Friday night, Cole was getting a drink at the bar, and he made eye contact with a stunning woman who was already staring at him. He smiled, and she shook her head in disappointment. Only then did Cole realize it was Mary Beth. She came over to him and said, "I thought we didn't have the same vocation."

Cole had noticed the engagement ring on her finger and said, "We don't. I'm in the seminary, but congratulations on yours."

Mary Beth raised her left hand in acknowledgement. "Thanks. Tonight is sort of my bachelorette party, but it's just me and my younger sister, Grace."

Mary Beth pointed her out, and seeing that she was dancing with Enzo, Cole said, "That's my roommate she's with."

Mary Beth giggled. "A seminarian? He may not be tomorrow. My sister's not like me. If she decides to change his vocation, she will."

Cole laughed, and they tried to continue their conversation, but the club was too loud. Mary Beth said, "Let's go outside so we can catch up."

Cole and Mary Beth talked for hours outside the club, and she was much different than Cole remembered. She no longer agreed with everything he said, but was thoughtful and nuanced in her opinions. To Cole, it was the most satisfying evening that he had ever spent with her.

At 3:00am, the club closed. Grace and Enzo exited together and were not ready to conclude their evening, so Mary Beth suggested, "Let's all go have breakfast."

Grace purred, "That's not what I had in mind."

Mary Beth intervened though. "I thought this was my bachelorette party, not yours."

At a nearby diner, Grace fell asleep waiting for her food. After the other three had eaten, Mary Beth advised, "Enzo, if you don't leave before she wakes up, you might do something you'll regret later." Cole laughed, but Enzo looked unsure which option he'd regret most.

Cole stood and took some money out to pay for breakfast, but Mary Beth stopped him. "My dad wouldn't want me to let seminarians pay for their meal. I'll tell him you said hi." Cole nodded in gratitude and nudged Enzo toward the door. Then, Cole looked back at Mary Beth. She was exquisite, both her body and her soul. Cole bit his lower lip so hard that he tasted blood, and said, "I hope for you the blessings of a long and fruitful marriage."

XIX.

During his time as pastor, Msgr. Steiner retrieved dozens of young men from the county jail, some more than once, and a few way too often. They usually wanted more than a ride home, assuming that Msgr.'s presence would calm parental wrath. They were also chagrined when Msgr. Steiner would ask to hear their confessions. It was never forced, but he almost always inquired. So, while Msgr. was not surprised when his phone rang at 3:00 am, he was shocked to hear Joseph Eldringhoff on the line.

When Joseph was sixteen years old, his father's arms had been caught and pulled into a hay baler. He regained some function of his left hand, but his right arm was too mutilated to be saved. So, Joseph quit school to operate the family farm. He was a hard worker, built like an ox from manual labor, and his face was weathered. Like the Steiners, the Eldringhoffs were a founding family of St. Hubertus, with a stained glass window in the church memorializing their contribution. Msgr. Steiner knew Joseph to be a responsible and pious young man, and could not understand how he would have ended up in jail.

Msgr. spoke with a deputy about the incident while waiting for Joseph to be released. He learned that Joseph was involved in a brawl at Frau's Haus. Similar incidents had occurred nearly every deer season for generations. Hunters from St. Louis would infest the area, and it was customary for them, during the evenings, to drink in the local establishments. For the most part, they were good guys with local family connections and farms. Some though were simply miscreants looking for fights and as often as not, they picked fights with local men who, for their part, were annoyed at the influx of strangers.

Once they were in Msgr.'s truck, he asked, "You know one of those guys has to have his jaw wired and won't eat solid food for a month?"

"Msgr., I'm sorry, but I promise I was just defending myself. I wasn't drunk, I'd just had one drink when all you-know-what broke loose."

Msgr. responded in a soft tone, "I know you wouldn't start trouble."

"I just don't know my own strength sometimes."

Msgr. laughed a bit. "You know, I always found it funny how they called you Little Joe and your dad Big Joe, when you were already bigger than him in seventh grade.

"There was too much confusion about who people were talking to, so I just started going by Joseph when I was sixteen." After a small pause, Joseph asked, "Do I need to make a confession?"

"Didn't I just hear your confession last week?"

"Yes, but . . ."

"I'll hear your confession if you want, but don't waste your breath about tonight. They started a brawl and got what they deserved. I'll go talk to Judge Niedringhaus in the morning."

"How much trouble do you think I'm in?"

"Years ago, I saw Judge Niedringhaus break a man's nose. I'll remind him of that."

"Thanks."

After Msgr. reflected on that distant event, he recalled, "I was actually with your Aunt Annette that evening. Did you know that I almost asked her to marry me?"

"No sir."

"Things might have been a lot different for me." Msgr. paused to consider his life's course. "Your aunt's a handsome woman and a terrific cook." He eyed Joseph, "Do you have anyone in mind to marry?"

"No sir."

Msgr. yawned, then asked, "How old are you now?"

"Thirty-three."

"Do you want to be married and have a family?"

"Yes sir, I just haven't found the right girl."

"Don't get too hung up on the right girl. Find a girl that you want to make it work with, make sure she wants to make it work with you, and then make it work together." He saw Joseph's dubious look. "My point is that there isn't necessarily one correct path for you in life. The path is what you make of it. I'm content as a priest, and could've been just as happy or more so married to your aunt, but I don't feel sorry for myself that I didn't marry her, you see. I make the most of the vocation I chose."

They drove in silence until Joseph said, "There was another guy from St. Hubertus in the jail."

"Who was it?" Msgr. wondered whether he'd have to return to the jail that night.

"Last name was Beck, I believe."

"Which Beck?" Even though Cole was supposed to be in St. Louis, Msgr. still wanted to be sure it wasn't him.

"I don't know, but he had a tattoo of the Ace of Spades on his forearm."

Msgr. grumbled, "That's Boone." He loathed even saying the name. "Was he part of this dust up at Frau's tonight?"

Joseph shrugged, "I don't think so."

Msgr. wondered about the nature of Boone's crime, and then spoke his mind to Joseph. "That creature is married to my niece."

"Sounds like you don't much care for him."

"He's a terrible person, and a worse husband." Msgr. squinted from the lights of an oncoming vehicle.

Joseph asked, "Since they're married, could you support her leaving him?"

"She knows I would, but she's just not yet ready to admit this was a mistake."

"I'm sorry she's having a difficult time."

"Thanks, but in addition to being prideful and stubborn, she's tough and resourceful, so this ordeal will only last as long as she lets it."

As they arrived at Eldringhoff Farm, Joseph asked, "What's your niece's name?"

"Jen."

"I'll pray that things work out for her. "

Msgr. knew that these weren't just meaningless words from Joseph and he was grateful. "Thanks, now go in and get some sleep."

Joseph responded with a smile, "Sleep? I'm already late starting my farm work."

"Good boy."

"Thanks for picking me up, Msgr."

"This time it was actually my pleasure."

XX.

Cole was lonely during Christmas of 2003. Most of his colleagues were gone, visiting their families during the break, and Cole remained at the seminary. He thought about Jen, and how he had never forgiven her. He also had not forgiven himself for pushing her out of his life when she needed his friendship the most. Jen had called him, sent him letters, and emailed him countless times since the day she had told him she was pregnant, but he had ignored her, and Cole now regretted being so cruel. So, one day Cole found the most recent email from Jen and hit reply. He typed, "Merry Christmas to you and your boys. I would like to send them each a gift. What is your address? Cole."

Jen's reply was quick and sassy. "Good to hear from you, finally. We're at the farm. Same trailer, ugh…"

This simple email exchange softened Cole's heart and relieved him of an ongoing burden. After a volley of emails, Cole was optimistic that their relationship was salvageable. Cole crafted his emails to Jen, so they were friendly, but shallow. He preferred to leave his wounds scabbed, for a while. Jen expedited their reconciliation though, emailing Cole, "I have an appointment in St. Louis on Friday. Can we meet for lunch?" Although apprehensive, Cole accepted the invitation.

On Friday, Cole thought that he had arrived first at the restaurant and took a seat. But then, there Jen was, standing at his table. She said, "You didn't recognize me."

Cole lied, "I hadn't even looked for you yet."

Jen appeared nothing like the slightly built teenager Cole remembered. She was womanly now, and Cole noticed her figure. In the past, Cole's attraction to Jen had very little to do with her looks. She had been a plain girl, and could not afford the benefits of fashionable clothes or a professional hair style. Cole remembered being asked by that older bartender, when he poured his heart out to her, if Jen was pretty, and not knowing how to respond. He had never thought about it. To him, she was just Jen, and that was plenty.

Jen took a seat and Cole was relieved to avoid the issue of whether they would shake hands or embrace in some way. After some catching up while they ate, Cole asked Jen about the appointment that had brought her to town. Jen responded, "You were my only appointment."

Relieved, Cole replied, "Oh. I was worried about your health since you needed to come all the way to St. Louis."

"I really needed to see you because I'm going through a lot right now."

"Does it have to do with why you are not wearing your ring? Are you guys splitting up?"

"In a way, maybe for a while. The ring is evidence though, it's being held by the police."

"Evidence of what?"

"Evidence that Boone is a criminal. He got busted stealing from homes he was remodeling. He took that ring from a house he was working on back in '97."

Cole was shocked and not shocked all at the same time. "What's he facing?"

"Years…, but the prosecutor offered him a deal that would have him out quick with a felony and a suspended sentence because they want him to testify about the others involved."

"Wow, how many people does it take to poach a few things from a house?"

"That was just a side thing that Boone did. Mainly, he sold information about the houses, like who lived there, when they came and went, and what they had worth stealing. The others would take that information and break in later on, so it wouldn't seem related to the remodel."

Cole shook his head, "He was destined for a life of crime, but never had the ambition or wit to be anything other than the errand boy. I'm even less surprised that he'd roll over on the others to get himself out of trouble."

"But I'm scared of what could happen if he does." Jen was trembling, "They are dangerous people."

"Then he shouldn't do it."

Jen asked, "How will I support my boys with him locked up?"

Cole was sympathetic and asked, "Is there something I can do?"

Jen's voice wavered as she spoke, "I just need you to be there for me, like you used to be." Not wanting to be seen crying in public, Jen got up to leave, and Cole followed her to the parking lot. She got into her minivan and unlocked the passenger door for Cole. Cole took a seat and waited for Jen to compose herself.

"Okay, I can do that, for today anyway."

Cole let Jen talk, and she had so much to say that the sun set, and the restaurant closed while they sat in the parking lot. When she finished, Jen leaned over to kiss Cole in appreciation. He smiled wryly at the bizarre circumstances of this, their first kiss. Jen smiled back and kissed him again, but this time more sensually. They stared at each other in silence for a moment. Then, Jen got out of the van and opened the sliding door. She tossed aside a booster seat and some toys to make space, then asked, "Are you waiting for an engraved invitation?"

Cole had missed her sense of humor and smiled. He joined Jen in the back seat, and they had sex, but it was cumbersome and over quickly.

Over the next week, Cole's roommate, Enzo, noticed that something was wrong. Cole was restless at night and despondent by day. And when Cole declined to go along on their regular Friday evening outing, Enzo said, "I'm worried about you, brother."

Cole replied, "Me too." He walked over to their door and shut it. "Last Friday, I saw my brother's wife."

"Doing what?

"No, I was with her." Enzo still didn't seem to understand, so Cole waited until Enzo figured it out.

"Oh my, that's not good."

Adding context, Cole explained, "He did steal her from me."

"She was your girlfriend?"

"No, but she should've been."

Enzo then asked, "Did you do it for revenge?"

Cole shook his head, "No."

"To sabotage their marriage?"

Cole repeated, "No."

"Then why?"

"I don't know." Cole thought for a moment about the truthful answer to Enzo's question before adding, "I do know that I have to leave Missouri because a hundred miles is not enough distance between us." Cole took a bag from the closet and started to pack.

"Where will you go?"

"The Army."

Enzo walked over to Cole and put his hand on his shoulder, "Go to confession before you leave."

Cole took a deep breath and considered. Then he said, "I can't because I'm unrepentant."

XXI.

Msgr. had dinner at the Big House on Sunday evenings with Grandma, Sister, and the spinsters. This time, Jen and the boys joined them. As usual, Grandma asked about Cole. Msgr. beamed and said, "He's doing really well at seminary." Jen set down her fork, closed her eyes, and took no more bites of food.

The next day, Jen stopped by the rectory. Msgr. welcomed her inside and said, "This is a pleasant surprise."

Jen responded, "You won't think so after you hear what I have to say." She paused for a deep breath and said, "Cole's gone. He left the seminary."

"What? How do you know?" Msgr. was shocked, he'd heard nothing from Cole in weeks.

"We've been emailing, and I went to St. Louis to see him."

"Well, where is he?" Msgr. was still processing the information, but now he was worried.

"I don't know, 'the Army' is all he said."

"This doesn't make any sense." Now thinking out loud, Msgr. rambled, "Doesn't he watch the news? These senseless wars…. Does he have a death wish?" Then, Msgr. put his left hand over his mouth and looked at Jen for a moment before asking, "Did you do something?" Jen's face turned pale as she eased towards the door, so he pressed her, "What did you do?"

Jen's body trembled as she shook her head.

Msgr. demanded an answer, "What did you do?"

Jen was panting now trying to catch her breath, and when she could, she begged. "I think you know. Please don't make me say it."

Msgr. turned away from his niece and roared, "God damn it!" and in a burst of anger he swiped a stack of newspaper off the table, scattering them about the floor.

Jen and Msgr. stood in the hollow stillness until Jen whimpered, "I'm sorry," and left.

The next morning, Msgr. sent one simple email to Cole. It read, "My son, remember, you will either receive God's justice or his mercy. You determine which one. In Christ, Msgr." Cole never responded, and Msgr. Steiner did not follow up.

XXII.

Jen emailed Cole often, and he responded sometimes. He could have responded more than he did, but considered it in their best interest to maintain both physical and emotional distance. Although, one particular email got a near instantaneous reply. In it, Jen noted, "Boone and I are expecting a baby. He accepted the plea deal hoping to be released in time for the birth."

Cole panicked, trying to calculate, using the limited information he had, whether he may be the father of this baby. Cole would not ask Jen directly though, as he was unwilling to memorialize their affair in an email. Instead, he replied with what he hoped was a subtle and innocuous follow up. "Jen, I hope this is a relief for you. When will he be home? When is the baby due? By the way, has he been away the whole time since his arrest?"

With a terse reply, Jen ignored Cole's questions, but addressed his obvious concern. "Cole, Boone and I are expecting. Be safe, Jen"

Cole had enough on his mind with a looming deployment to Iraq, so he took her word for it.

XXIII.

Cole was a good soldier and proud to serve, but he witnessed first-hand the tumult of Iraq in 2005 and quickly lost passion for the mission. Later in life, he questioned the prudence of overthrowing the Ba'athist regime of Saddam Hussein in the first place, and even, if he had a sympathetic audience, went so far as to call the war unjust and a violation of international law. While in uniform, however, Cole quietly did his duty.

Cole managed to escape Iraq physically unscathed, and with only the expected amount of psychological damage. During his deployment, Cole was exposed to gruesome realities. He witnessed grotesque injury and death involving his compatriots and civilians, including children. To his knowledge, he did not kill anyone in combat. He did though, strike a woman with his Humvee while fleeing an IED attack. Unsure of her fate, Cole presumed she died. He relived the incident in a recurrent dream for years, but never considered it a symptom of PTSD, just the natural byproduct of ending a human life.

Cole returned home numb. Now ambivalent toward organized religion, Cole's time in the seminary, though only a couple years past, seemed like another lifetime. He was able to fulfill the remainder of his enlistment commitment with Missouri National Guard. He took up residence in Jefferson City and worked for a tree care service. Cole and Jen half-heartedly agreed to meet at some point, but neither pressed to set a date.

XXIV.

Cole first heard about the local shootout on the national news. "Overnight, three armed men forced their way into a trailer near Jefferson City, Missouri, terrorizing a young family. Two people were fatally shot, one suspect is still at large, and one arrest has been made. Authorities are withholding the names of both the victims and suspects."

Not long after seeing the news story, Cole received a text from Jen: "Did you hear about the shooting?"

    Cole texted: Yes.
    Jen texted: Boone's been arrested. Can you come here?
    Cole texted: I'm on my way.

On the short drive, Cole considered that the last time he had been in St. Hubertus was 1997, nine years prior. He also took a moment to remember the boys' names and birth order. The first two were easy, Bo and Hunter. Fairly certain that the third was called Shooter, he realized he had no idea what the fourth was named, and since Jen had surely told him, he didn't want to ask.

Jen was alone in the trailer with just the baby when Cole arrived. He was still learning to walk and toddled over to Cole, who got down on his knees and took a close look at the child. Jen sassed Cole when she noticed him staring at the baby. "Do you really think I wouldn't have told you if this was your baby?" Cole was afraid to answer, sure that whatever he did say would not lead to a productive discussion. Realizing he wouldn't answer, Jen added, "I may have slept with my husband's brother, but I'm not a monster."

Cole had always admired the way she wielded words, but in this case, preferred to change the subject. "So, what happened?"

"Boone shot the men that broke into the trailer."

"What? This trailer?" He looked around for signs of damage.

"No, his girlfriend's trailer."

"Oh." Cole had not expected that news, but wasn't shocked either. "And the kids they mentioned on the news?"

"His with her, apparently."

"How long have you known?"

"About an hour."

"Jen, I'm sorry."

"Don't be. It's like winning the lottery as far as I'm concerned. If he wasn't over there, it would've happened here."

"What do you mean?"

"The police caught the one that got away. They went there to kill Boone and any witnesses. These are his house robbery buddies he turned on to get that reduced sentence."

"But wait, doesn't that make it self-defense? Why was he arrested?"

"I'm trying to understand that myself, but the police said it's murder because felons can't own guns."

Cole stayed for a couple hours, but left before the older boys returned. He asked Jen to keep him informed and told her he would help with whatever she needed. Jen felt strangely unburdened, especially considering that in that one day, she learned that her husband had survived a murder attempt, had children with another woman, and could be going to prison for years or even decades. However, when Boone did not return home after he was released pending his trial, she was soon overwhelmed by the responsibility of supporting their children alone.

XXV.

The Law Offices of James T. Ward and Associates was a misnomer. It was only one office, in a suburban St. Louis strip mall, and there were no associates. There was not even a receptionist. Jimmy did the best he could with the general practice he had, but the cases did not pay well, and he often waived his fee to help clients who were truly in need. With his practice failing and a third child on the way, Jimmy had accepted that working for his father in law was an inevitability when he and Lillian first heard about Boone Beck on the evening news.

During the commercial break, Lillian asked, "Why would there be murder charges if he was defending himself and his children in his own home?"

Jimmy thought it through out loud. "If someone dies during the commission of a felony, it's second degree murder. And because of the shooter's record, just possessing the gun he used is a felony."

"That's ridiculous."

"I know, and I think an argument can be made that the Second Amendment enshrines an absolute right to keep and bear arms in self-defense, even for convicted felons."

As Jimmy thought more about Boone's story that evening, he began to relive a traumatic experience from his own childhood that he had repressed for many years. Lillian noticed the shift in his mood and asked, "Is something bothering you?"

"Yeah. Something that I'd forgotten about, an incident when I was a kid." With a blank stare, Jimmy told the story for the first time in his life. "Someone knocked on our door and I answered it. Two men forced their way passed me. My mom was in the kitchen and didn't know what was happening until it was too late."

When Jimmy stopped, Lillian asked, "What was happening?"

Still looking away from his wife, Jimmy answered, "One held my mom on the ground while the other ransacked the house."

"What did you do?"

"Cowered in the corner until they left."

Lillian moved closer to Jimmy and hugged him.

Jimmy added, "We didn't have much worth stealing, but they took what little sense of security I had."

Still hugging Jimmy, Lillian said "You should be thankful that it didn't end worse with you and your mom, living there alone." Then, she suggested, "Maybe you should help this guy if you can."

Jimmy thought about it overnight, and by morning was invigorated by the possibility. So, using the online court database, Jimmy confirmed that Boone Beck was unrepresented at his arraignment and jotted down his listed address. That same day, Jimmy drove to St. Hubertus to find Boone and pitch his theory of the case. Jimmy parked near the gate to Steiner Farm and started on foot toward the several buildings he could see in the distance. He was surprised to find himself walking through a Christmas tree farm. Passing the field of Scotch Pines, Jimmy thought about the Christmases of his youth. He remembered wondering why Santa Claus was more generous with his ill-behaved cousins, when they already had so much. Then, as he aged, he resented his mother for not being able to give him more, even knowing that she had to buy him gifts on layaway. As he grew up, he felt shame for these feelings towards his mother knowing the sacrifices she had made to give him what little she did. But instead of appreciating his mother's altruism as being in the true spirit of Christmas, Jimmy was embittered by the materialism of the season, often chastising his children for asking for presents and questioning his wife for indulging them. He was jolted from his reflections by a loud gruff voice.

"Boone's not here." Jimmy halted, surprised by the voice coming from the field. Looking through the trees, he saw a man in a flannel shirt coming toward him. When Jimmy didn't respond, the man followed up, "Is that not why you're here?"

"It is. How did you know?"

"Lots of people are looking for Boone; investigators, reporters, and lawyers."

Disappointed to learn he wasn't the only attorney interested in Boone's case, Jimmy answered in a defeated tone, "That's me, just another lawyer."

"Well, counselor, Boone's not here and I don't care to know where he is. His wife lives in that trailer over there, and you're welcome to ask her yourself, but I can save you the trouble. She doesn't know where he is either."

Jimmy responded, "Thanks for your time," but lingered, staring at the Christmas trees.

The man asked, "Is there something else I can help you with?"

"I was just wondering about the trees. Can you make a living selling them?"

"I wouldn't know, it's just a hobby for me. My vocation is shepherd."

"They're beautiful. Is it a lot of work or do they grow like this on their own?"

"Some are no work at all, but others need lots of care. Some though, will never look good, no matter what I do."

"I don't see any ugly ones."

"That's because each of those has been culled, mulched, and replaced by a sapling."

Jimmy took another moment to admire the Christmas trees before refocusing, "Thanks for your help, but I'd still like to speak with the wife, if possible."

Gesturing toward the trailer, the man replied, "Suit yourself."

The trailer was a short walk from the Christmas tree field and Jimmy only made it about two thirds of the way before hearing a familiar mantra, "Boone's not here." This time it came from a female voice that poured out through the screen door and open windows of the trailer. Undeterred, Jimmy drew closer to it. The woman emerged and stood on the porch, keeping the high ground.

"You're right, I did come for Boone, but I'm here now to speak with you about him."

"He's not my favorite subject these days."

"I understand that."

"No, I don't think you can."

Jen turned and opened the screen door to signal the end of the conversation, but Jimmy persisted, "You resent most that he left you here with no way to support your children." Jen kept her back to Jimmy but stayed in the doorway. So, he continued, "I can help you with that."

Jen turned to face Jimmy and stepped out again, letting the door close behind her. "How?"

"He's far more valuable to you out of prison and earning a living, and I can minimize his time away." Jimmy took out a business card as he approached the porch and handed it to Jen.

Jen read the card and said "Alright James, I'll pass your information along if I hear from him.

Within the week, Jimmy heard from Boone and came back to central Missouri to meet him at a bar at the Lake of the Ozarks. They discussed the case over drinks. Jimmy explained, "We can fight the murder charges, but we'll most likely lose at trial. Then, on appeal, we'll argue that your actions in self-defense are protected by the Second Amendment."

Boone's opinion was unequivocal. "Any prison time is bullshit."

Jimmy replied, "I agree, but you may be incarcerated during the appeal, and there's no guarantee of a successful outcome."

"How much will it cost?"

"I won't charge you for my services."

First hopeful, then skeptical, Boone replied, "Why?"

"Because I don't think you did anything wrong."

Boone thought for a moment, then said, "I've talked to some lawyers and you're the only one who'll fight the murder charges and do it for free." So, Boone signed a stack of papers authorizing Jimmy to start work on his case.

The next day, Jimmy filed his entry of appearance on Boone's behalf and touched base with the prosecutor. After brief introductions and minimal pleasantries, Jimmy asked, "Are you hell-bent on sticking with the murder charges or can we negotiate our way out of them?"

The prosecutor didn't budge. "I'm sorry, but there's too much public interest in discouraging criminals from arming themselves."

With more sass than he intended, Jimmy answered. "What about the public interest in discouraging criminals from breaking into homes and terrorizing children?"

"I'm aware of the mitigating circumstances of the case." The prosecutor sounded annoyed, but softened her voice before adding, "And that's why I'll recommend leniency to the judge if your clients pleads guilty."

"A lenient sentence on double murder?"

"That's right, your client would serve years instead of decades."

"For defending himself and his children in his own home?" Jimmy waited for a response, but the prosecutor said nothing in tacit affirmation. "We're going to pass."

XXVI.

During Boone's first incarceration, Jen had relied on public assistance. Now though, with Boone wrapped up in a legal battle and facing the possibility of a longer sentence, Msgr. Steiner and Sister Paul Joseph colluded to help Jen. They offered her a job as a teacher's assistant in the St. Hubertus preschool, even allowing her to bring her youngest along with her while she worked. With Bo in second grade, Hunter in Kindergarten, and Shooter in preschool, all attending St. Hubertus, she could be near her children while earning some money. Jen accepted, but feared that the job alone would not be enough to sustain the family.

That December, Msgr. Steiner pulled up to Jen's trailer with two Christmas trees in the bed of his truck. He removed one that was modest in size and perfect in shape, and carried it inside. The boys were excited about the tree because they knew it meant Santa Claus was coming soon. With the tree set in its stand, Msgr. Steiner returned to his truck, took four Cokes from a cooler, gave three to the older boys, and kept one for himself. The boys scattered with their drinks and Jen and Msgr. Steiner stood together quietly for a while.

"How are you feeling?" Msgr. asked Jen.

"Alone." She didn't seem sad about it, just telling the truth.

"Do not fear, God is always with you. He will strengthen you, help you, and uphold you with his righteous hand."

"Those words are nice, but they don't solve my problems."

"But the people who believe those words do solve problems."

Msgr. Steiner reached into the pocket of his flannel shirt, removed an envelope stuffed with cash, and handed it to Jen. "Your fellow parishioners wanted you to feel loved and supported."

Without waiting for a response from the speechless Jen, Msgr. Steiner got into his truck to leave. "Alright," he said, "I better get this other tree up to the Big House. Your grandmother made cinnamon rolls and I would like to get one while they're still warm."

As Msgr.'s truck lumbered toward the big house, Jen considered his use of the words, "fellow parishioners." Jen considered herself a Catholic, even though for many years she had not acted like one. She witnessed the baptism of her children and went to church for other important occasions, but had long ago stopped going to Sunday mass, citing the difficulty of bringing small children. Sister Paul Joseph, however, came to the trailer every Sunday and Holy Day. Leaving any nursling with Jen, she took the other boys to mass, just as she had done with Jen.

Sometime after that Christmas, Sister Paul Joseph was away at a conference for Catholic school principals. Bo and Hunter had dressed themselves for Sunday mass, but Jen said, "Change into play clothes. Sister is out of town, so you're not going to church today."

"Why can't we still go?" said Bo.

Hunter chimed in with the legalism of all six-year olds. "It's Sunday. Sunday is church day."

Jen didn't want to go, but she would for her sons. "Fine. We'll go."

Jen found something to wear, rushed through a shower, and did just enough with her hair and makeup to go into public. She considered it a small miracle that they were not late. Jen and the boys took seats in a pew with Grandma Steiner, the spinsters, Aunt Josephine, and Uncle Pius.

The children, well catechized for their ages, behaved better than Jen expected, and after mass, Jen was surprised to find herself enjoying talking to people. Parishioners, some familiar and some strangers, aware of her circumstances, offered support and words of encouragement. Also, some preschool parents approached Jen, and thanked her for caring for their children in school.

That evening, as Jen was putting the boys to bed, Hunter asked, "Will you come to church with us every week, mommy?"

She had no excuses that she was willing to share with her young son, and replied, "I will."

The first two weeks, Jen did not even consider going up to receive Communion. She knew Msgr. Steiner would not have offered her Communion even if she had. She needed to confess her sins first. She had confessed to Msgr. Steiner many times before, but that was as a child, and even though he should already assume most of what she had to say, she found she simply could not tell him everything.

Instead, Jen went to the confession in the nearby hamlet of St. Barnabas. Fr. Bob heard confessions from 3:30-3:45 every Saturday afternoon prior to the vigil mass at St. Barnabas church. When Jen opened the church door, she was relieved to find it empty. She hoped that Fr. Bob had cancelled confession; she was willing to procrastinate another week.

Before she could leave though, a man wearing sandals, chinos, and an untucked oxford shirt appeared. Watering can in hand, he was attempting to save the few remaining Christmas poinsettias, but the leaves were already wilted. He saw Jen and asked, "Are you here for confession?"

"Yeah, but if Father Bob is unavailable, I'll come back next time."

"I am Father Bob. Have a seat and we'll get you fixed up.

"Right here in the pew?"

"We can go to the confessional, if you want, but we're the only ones here and I've already seen you, so anonymity shouldn't be a concern."

"Okay, but I have a lot, so it may take a bit." Jen took a seat in the pew and Fr. Bob sat next to her.

"Surely not, you look like a nice young woman."

"Well, it's been a decade or so."

"Since you already told me how long it's been, proceed with your sins."

After a pause to gather herself, Jen started with the least salacious of her mortal sins. "I missed almost every mass for ten years. I received the Eucharist unworthily…"

Father Bob interrupted. "Unworthily? You were still one of God's children, no? Would a father not feed his child, even if she'd been unruly?"

Unsure how to answer, Jen attempted to press forward. "I have a lot of sexual sins." The thought of them had her on the verge of tears, and she tried to fight them back.

Fr. Bob interrupted again, "I see that you are very upset, but know that God wants you to be happy. There is no need to continue. I believe that you are very sorry for your sins, and they will be forgiven."

"But I have more."

"And you will be absolved of them as well." Jen wrinkled her brow, but made no further objection as Fr. Bob continued. "For your penance, say a prayer of your choice." Fr. Bob then finished with the prayer of absolution.

Jen stopped at Msgr. Steiner's cabin on her way home. Unlike most of his colleagues, Msgr. did not offer a vigil mass, refusing to indulge those who wanted "to get mass out of the way on Saturday." Jen found him among his Christmas trees, pruning those that needed it, and admiring those that did not.

"Uncle Gus, Christmas is long way off."

"Every tree still in this field was not chosen last Christmas. Some are good as is, but it just wasn't the right time. I can nurture others, improving their chances to be picked next season. Some though, will never be good enough, no matter how I help them. Those, I will bring to the wood chipper, and the school playground will have fresh mulch."

Changing the subject, Jen announced, "I went to confession at St. Barnabas."

"I'm glad that you went, but I want you to know that you can always come to me to confess your sins." Msgr. Steiner nudged his flock away from St. Barnabas at every opportunity, unimpressed by what he thought of as Fr. Bob's "renditions of the sacraments."

"You wouldn't want to hear what I had to say."

"Of course not, I'm queasy just thinking about it. But that's irrelevant, I would endure immense discomfort to ensure that you, or any of my spiritual children, are spared eternal damnation."

"I just wanted you to know before I came to communion tomorrow."

After a brief pause, Msgr. asked, "Do you remember what I told you at your First Communion?"

"Of course, 'the Eucharist is all that matters.'"

Msgr. nodded in approval. "I'm impressed you remembered."

"You've told every First Communion class the same thing for forty years."

"It's been true for a lot longer than that."

XXVII.

Jen texted:	Bo has a family history project for school and questions about your family. Would you be willing to meet him and help?
Cole texted:	Definitely.
Jen texted:	Thanks. What works best for you?
Cole texted:	Bring them all to Jefferson City Saturday? Meet at McDonald's for lunch?
Jen texted:	See you then.

Cole beat Jen to the restaurant this time, and grabbed a large table near the play area. He spotted Jen's minivan pulling into a parking space and had an unexpected emotional reaction. Cole felt himself swelling with guilt, watching his nephews exit the minivan while considering what he had done with their mother therein. Cole knew that once he met his nephews, his life would change forever. He could no longer go on acting as though they didn't exist, and would be duty bound to take responsibility for them.

Jen skipped formal introductions, seated the older boys at the table, and took the smallest child to order food. Cole stopped her. "Let me go, so I can pay."

Jen insisted though, "The order is too hard to explain. It'll help me more if you just make sure the boys stay somewhere near the table."

While Jen ordered the food, Cole turned to the oldest who was nine. "Bo, right?"

Bo agreed.

He turned to the seven-year old, "Hunter, yes?"

Hunter nodded. "Uh, huh."

The third brother was four, "Is your name Shooter?"

Unnerved to be without his mother and left with a stranger, Shooter stared back at Cole in silence.

Bo said, "That's his name."

"Bo, can you answer a question for me, but not tell your mom I asked it?"

"Sister Paul Joseph says to never trust an adult that asks you to keep a secret."

Impressed, Cole admitted, "That's really good advice. How about I ask you the question, you answer it, and then you decide whether you should tell your mom?"

"Okay."

"What is your youngest brother's name?"

Bo answered, "Archer."

When Jen came back to the table, Cole made a point to call Archer by name. Jen smiled when he did, and then interrogated the children playfully. "Who told him?"

Cole kidded Jen, "Told who what?" He then winked at Bo and Bo winked back. Hunter giggled, and Shooter followed suit.

After lunch, the boys made use of the play area. Jen and Cole tried to talk, but it was difficult, with regular interruptions for disciplinary purposes. They did, however, briefly discuss the most significant development in Jen's life. "Boone and I are getting divorced."

Cole felt something stir inside him, "That's probably warranted, considering…"

"We might have survived the side family, but he abandoned our children and stopped supporting them. I can't get past that."

Just then, Archer returned to his mother, frustrated that some of the attractions in the play area were too advanced for him. Jen comforted and redirected him. To Cole, her maneuver seemed effortless, like an instinctive reflex. Cole was charmed watching Jen in the role of mother, and even a bit aroused. He never forgot that Grandma Steiner had said that Jen, "will be a good wife to the right man" and blamed Boone, the wrong man, for her infidelity.

Cole excused himself to get some items from his truck. He gave Bo an envelope of family pictures to help with his project and each of the boys a trinket that once belonged to their grandmother. Cole could not remember the last time that he felt so buoyed up by kinship, or if he ever had.

Cole texted Jen that same night.

Cole texted: Thanks for today. I really enjoyed hanging out with the boys.

Jen texted: No Cole, thank you for being there for us.

Cole texted: I want to plan something else with the boys, but think that we should meet without them first.

Jen texted: Like a date?

Cole texted: Like two adults eating dinner and talking about their future.

Jen texted: That sounds like a date.

Cole texted: Call it what you want, but it's long overdue. I'd like to have a better understanding of where things stand between us.

Jen texted: Friday night? Jefferson City?

Cole texted: Great, I'll figure out where and let you know.

At the restaurant, the young couple was stylishly dressed and dining sans children. Jen observed, "The waiter thinks this is a date." Then, she chuckled, "It would be my first ever."

"Really?" Cole was surprised by Jen's admission.

"I don't think getting knocked up in my mom's trailer counts, and that was Boone's magnum opus in romance."

Cole didn't know whether he should laugh. Her statement was funny, but the underlying pain was palpable. "What are you going to do with Boone out of the picture?"

"I'm working at the preschool, and I get some help from Msgr. and Sister.

He should have expected Msgr. Steiner would be helping Jen, she was his niece after all, but hearing his former mentor's name made Cole uneasy. Cole had no reasonable excuse for ignoring Msgr. Steiner for three years. He had gone to war and returned without even a cursory update for the man who had treated him as a son. Cole realized he had been thinking of Jen as somehow apart from St. Hubertus and Msgr. Steiner, but with a sober mind, Cole knew they were inseparable.

Cole cleared his throat. "How is Msgr.?"

"He would like to hear from you."

Cole said, "I know," and then changed the subject. "When I asked what you were going to do, you told me how you would support your family. I was more interested in you, personally."

"There's no difference when you have children."

"That's fair… and I want to help you with the boys."

"In what way?"

"You know, just be there for you guys." Cole tested Jen's appetite for a relationship.

"You want to be an uncle?"

"More than that."

"You want to be a father to them?" Most of all, Cole had missed Jen's directness.

"I guess I do."

"What about me?" Jen rephrased her question to be clear. "What do you want to be to me?"

"For half my life, I've wanted to be with you. Did you really need to ask?"

Jen considered his proposition before responding. "Cole, I love you, but I can't rush into a relationship with you. I need to be a better example for my boys than my mother was for me."

"I understand that."

"But I want you to come around and get to know them better, and if something develops between us, I'm open to that. If that happens though, it's important to me that my boys don't see what I did as a kid, so you have to leave before they go to bed, and there won't be any sex unless we get married."

Unbeknownst to Jen, Cole had lived as a de facto celibate since their minivan encounter, so it wouldn't be the sacrifice for him that she expected. "I can live with that."

"There is one last thing… You need to get my uncle's blessing."

"Which uncle?"

"You know which one, don't be a smart ass."

Cole didn't want to, but he would. "If marriage becomes a real possibility, I will go talk to him, for you."

Jen corrected Cole. "For us."

XXVIII.

Joseph Eldringhoff eventually married. His bride, Maria, was a nurse at a doctor's office in Jefferson City. Joseph first met her years earlier at one of his father's regular appointments. Thereafter, Joseph insisted on accompanying his father to every appointment.

Not long after they were married, Joseph and Maria learned that they were expecting twins. At the advice of her doctor, Maria stopped taking medication that she had used most of her adult life for headaches. Without it, Maria was soon incapacitated several days per week. At her next appointment, Maria asked her doctor, "Is there something safe that I can take instead."

The doctor advised, "Probably, but it would help to know the cause of the headaches, so we should start with an MRI."

After the MRI, Joseph and Maria met with a neurologist, who said, "You have a brain tumor, and it's inoperable. There are other treatments available, but they are not safe for the fetuses."

Maria responded, "Then I'll wait until after they're born."

As the pregnancy progressed, so did the tumor. Maria's pain increased, and her faculties waned. Her doctors scheduled a meeting with Joseph. The hospital's administrator and general counsel attended as well, concerned about the ethical and legal issues involved.

The oncologist led the meeting stating, "There may still be time to treat the tumor, but the window is closing."

Joseph answered, "That's not what she wants to do."

The neurologist then suggested, "She may no longer have the capacity to make this type of medical decision."

All present looked at Joseph for a response. "Let me talk to her and I'll let you know." Joseph would not sway Maria in either direction, but preferred to save his wife. He figured that they could have more babies later, but only if she recovered.

When Joseph found Maria in a moment of lucidity, he told her what the doctors had said. She insisted, "Don't let them hurt our babies." Joseph was struck by Maria's use of the words "our babies." While he had not yet considered himself a parent, Maria did.

At his next meeting with the doctors and administrators, Joseph declared, "Maria's decision is to be respected."

The oncologist was imperious. "That's called suicide."

"It's not suicide," Joseph told him, "it's motherhood."

When Maria's organs began failing in their thirtieth week of gestation, the obstetrician convinced Joseph that the babies were now safer outside of their mother. It was too late to save Maria though. Msgr. Steiner travelled to the hospital and gave Maria the sacrament of Anointing of the Sick. Then, in the NICU, Msgr. baptized and confirmed Gianna and Chiara Eldringhoff, with a nurse functioning as godmother.

Afterward, Msgr. spoke to a despairing Joseph. "Take comfort knowing that she'll rest at the bosom of Abraham." Joseph did not respond, so Msgr. continued. "This won't be easy for you. Please, do not lose your faith."

Joseph then responded, "I don't know if I can do this alone."

"You won't have to. You'll always have the support of your parish family."

After eleven weeks in the hospital, the twins went home with their father. He had help from the girls' grandmothers as well as fellow parishioners, but not all the time. He did his best, but struggled.

XXIX.

Leading up to Boone's trial, Jimmy took his case straight to the American people. He publicized the case, appearing on talk shows and news outlets. He would ask, "Do we as a nation believe that a non-violent felon is so irredeemable that he forever cedes his right to defend himself and family with firearms?"

During one cable news appearance, Jimmy met a co-panelist who went by what he presumed to be a pseudonym, Madison James. Madison was a darling of libertarian social media, but it was clear to Jimmy that she put herself in the midst of controversy solely for self-promotion. She was a former Miss Texas who took the crown with an Annie Oakley style shooting performance in the talent competition. After her reign, Madison became even more famous for her series of firearms instructional videos. She was undeniably an expert on guns, but her body, chiseled by Pilates and hardened by jiu-jitsu, was the true star of the videos. As a television commentator, she had only a middling understanding of constitutional law, but she made up for it with her sharp tongue and intoxicating sex appeal.

When they finished taping their segment, Madison asked Jimmy, "Why don't we team up and make some money off this case."

Jimmy wasn't interested, but had just met Madison and indulged her to be polite. "What do you have in mind?"

"A website for my freedom loving fans. I'll make videos for it and you can write articles, or we could each do both."

"I already have a blog dedicated to the case."

Underwhelmed, Madison responded, "A blog? I'm taking about something much bigger."

"Look, I'm proud of the blog, and the support I've received from across the political spectrum. Both civil libertarians and criminal justice reformers are interested in the case, and I'm afraid that a partnership with you would alienate some of them."

Madison put a hand on each of his shoulders and looked into his eyes. "Who cares whether people like you or support what you're doing? I'm talking about making money."

Jimmy didn't have a good feeling about Madison's offer and trusted his instinct. "I'm sorry, but I'm not interested."

A week later, Madison contacted Jimmy with a formal proposal, complete with revenue models, and an offer sweetened in his favor. Astonished by the amount of money at stake, Jimmy said yes.

Soon after, the duo launched a gun rights website, thewellregulatedmilitia.com, as well as a companion periodical called *30 Round Magazine.* They offered updates about the case and articles by Jimmy and Madison on the Second Amendment, but most important to the bottom line, they had plenty of paid advertisements. They also sold merchandise, including shirts, coffee mugs, and bumper stickers.

While Madison had a rabid and devoted following, Jimmy was a far more artful messenger for the cause. Some of Jimmy's articles were picked up by national publications, which led to even more frequent television appearances. Soon, Jimmy's celebrity rivaled, if not exceeded, Madison's.

XXX.

Boone Beck's trial date loomed, and Jimmy, distracted by fame and money, lost enthusiasm for the case. He even began to question the prudence of his plan, as it became clear that Boone would probably not be able to avoid prison. Even a successful appeal could result in as much or more time behind bars as the deal the prosecutor already offered.

Only days before the trial, Jimmy received a voicemail from the prosecutor. Public opinion had swelled against the murder charges and Jimmy sensed that she wanted the case and accompanying media storm to go away. Jimmy planned to wait a day to return her call, so he could negotiate from a position of strength, but when she called again that afternoon, he answered, and she made an offer. "If your client pleads guilty to unlawful possession, I'll drop the murder charges and recommend no more than three years."

Jimmy pushed back, knowing that Boone would never agree to three years. "The recommendation is too high."

The prosecutor then buckled. "Fine, not more than one year."

"Okay, I'll talk to my client and let you know."

While it was in Boone's best interest to accept the offer, Jimmy was bound by ethics to get his consent first. But Boone balked at the deal and Jimmy found himself frustrated. "You knew going into this that prison time was likely during the appeal. That alone could be more than a year."

Boone snapped back. "You said that you could get me out of this and all you did was get yourself rich and famous."

"You wouldn't even have this deal if I hadn't made your case famous."

But that just infuriated Boone and he yelled through the phone, "You didn't do anything for me. You used me and now you're trying to walk away. At least if we have a trial, you'll have to do some actual work for all the money you've made off me."

Jimmy already felt guilty about the money. He knew he had made it off Boone's hardship. He knew he didn't deserve it. But he also knew that this plea deal was in Boone's best interest. So, Jimmy tried to force Boone's hand.

"You can accept this deal or not, but if you don't, I will withdraw from the case. With me and my fame no longer a concern to the prosecutor, I'd expect the deal to be pulled. You may or may not find a lawyer willing to represent you at trial and during a lengthy appeal without pay. Either way, your attorney, likely a public defender, will be there to do lots of work to get you released when and if they can convince an appeals court that it's good public policy for felons to be armed."

    Boone capitulated. The judge accepted the prosecutor's recommendation and Boone surrendered to custody. The outcome of the case was far better than Boone could have expected, but he nevertheless bemoaned ever hiring the "jackleg St. Louis lawyer."

XXXI.

The case went away, but Jimmy's celebrity did not. He became an icon for a growing following of gun nuts. They referred to themselves collectively as the Well-Regulated Militia. In public they recognized each other by shirts and bumper stickers purchased from the website and proudly waved to or visited with any fellow "militia" members they encountered.

The money and fame became too much for Jimmy to handle. He drank to excess almost daily, especially when away from home. On one trip, he met Madison in New York for a meeting with an advertising agency. They arrived separately the afternoon before the morning meeting and planned to meet for dinner after Madison's evening session of jiu-jitsu. Jimmy drank while Madison trained. They talked business early in the meal, but Jimmy was unclear what happened after that, except for some vivid, but intermittent memories of a sexual encounter with Madison in his hotel room.

In the morning, Jimmy awoke alone and there was no sign that Madison had ever been there. Jimmy was hung over and vomited. He took a shower, then vomited again. He struggled, but made it through the meeting. On their way out, he asked Madison, "Where were you this morning?"

She seemed confused by the question, and said, "Jiu-jitsu, I guess. Why?"

Jimmy found her answer odd, but let it go. Back at his hotel room, he questioned his memory. He wondered if it was a dream or even a drunken hallucination. Worried about his mental health, he scoured the room for any sign that she had been there. He found nothing to corroborate his memories. So, he got into the bed and closed his eyes trying to remember anything else from the prior night. Frustrated, he rolled onto his stomach, and noticed the pillow smelled like Madison.

The next morning, they shared a taxi to the airport. Jimmy asked Madison, "Should we talk about the other night?"

"What about it?"

"About what happened?"

"We ate at a restaurant."

"Is that all?" Jimmy could tell his questions annoyed Madison, but he needed some sort of closure.

"No, that's not all."

When Jimmy returned home, he was sick with regret. He stopped drinking for a while, but without the numbing effect of alcohol, Jimmy's troubled thoughts, about money, about fame, about what he was doing with his life, and now, the guilt from the affair, intruded on him all day and night. Sometimes Lillian and the children would speak to him and he wouldn't even notice, so he started drinking again to block out his thoughts. After some trial and error, he found the right combination of drink quantity and time of day to start, so he was best able to work and interact his family without becoming too drunk. Jimmy wouldn't drink in the mornings, but at noon, he'd fill a fourteen-ounce travel mug with vodka. He'd ration that pour until dinner, then he'd drink openly during the evenings.

Jimmy also drank before public appearances. One time, he agreed to appear on a cable news panel after a school shooting. Distraught by the massacre and anticipating tough questions from the host, Jimmy over imbibed before the segment. Live on air, the host asked Jimmy, "Is the well-regulated militia to blame for this tragedy?"

Jimmy barked, "No." He took off his earpiece, tossed it on the table, and walked off the set.

Jimmy turned off his cell phone and drank alone in his hotel room for the rest of the night. Late in the morning, Jimmy responded to pounding on the door. Madison pushed her way past him, and Jimmy said, "I'm sorry."

Smiling, Madison asked, "For what?"

"For that scene last night." Jimmy was dizzy from standing, so he made his way over to a chair.

Madison giggled, then said, "You don't know, do you? You went viral. All the networks and cable news shows are leading with it like you're some sort of deranged lunatic. But the militia loved it, and now we have lots of new supporters who think you were mistreated. We're running out of merchandise it's selling so fast. The idiots in the media don't realize that every time they say "well-regulated militia," we make money."

This news was overwhelming Jimmy, so he took a moment to process everything. Then, he asked, "Is it really worth it to you? To make money off this?"

"The kids are already dead, Jim. We're just making the most of a bad situation."

Jimmy put his face in his hands and rubbed his eyes. "I'm done with this," he said finally.

Madison didn't seem to understand what Jimmy meant and continued to talk business. "The NRA called this morning. They're so pissed we're getting this attention that they can't even shoot straight. They asked if we would entertain an offer to sell, but I told them, 'Hell no, we're getting richer by the minute.'"

Hoping Madison would understand this time, Jimmy said, "Well, I want to sell, at least my shares anyway."

"You own too much, Jim. If you sell, they'll control me, and I don't want to work for those assholes. So, we either both sell or not."

"Like I said, I'm done. So, you can buy my shares or someone else will."

Madison thought for a moment and conceded, "The business will never be worth more than it is today. I'll call the NRA."

XXXII.

For a while, Cole managed to both court Jen and avoid Msgr. Steiner. They almost never visited at her trailer, instead meeting outside the circle of the St. Hubertus rumor mill. It helped that the boys liked this better; outings usually meant some sort of treat or experience unavailable at home. However, Cole knew that he could not avoid Msgr. Steiner forever, and an encounter was all but assured when he agreed to accompany Jen and the boys to the St. Hubertus Day Festival.

In the early years of the parish, St. Hubertus Day began with a mass intended for the safety and bounty of the upcoming hunting season. After mass, a potluck feast of wild game and beer continued until sundown. These days though, St. Hubertus Day was more like a carnival, with game booths and food for purchase.

Some sharp-eyed St. Hubertus resident had noticed that Jägermeister's label portrayed a cross between antlers, and the parishioners had adopted it as the unofficial drink of St. Hubertus Day. Msgr. Steiner groused about the new tradition, not because of the excessive consumption of alcohol on a feast day, but because the label depicted a cross instead of a crucifix. In his homily every November 3, Msgr. would say, "Surely, St. Hubertus would have objected to the removal of Christ from the cross."

Cole met Jen and the boys at the festival after mass. Cole was shocked to find out how many parishioners remembered him, and fondly. They shook his hand and thanked him for his service. Some even asked him if he would still become a priest. Cole, as before, gave a noncommittal answer, but knew he was lying. He enjoyed the easy sense of community until he found himself smiling and waving to a familiar face before he realized it belonged to Msgr. Steiner. They made eye contact, but did not speak to each other. That evening, Jen told Cole, "You're going to have to talk to him sometime." He replied, "I know."

XXXIII.

Msgr. Steiner had adhered to the same weekday morning regimen for four decades. He spent the six o'clock hour in prayer before the Blessed Sacrament and the first half of the seven o'clock hour saying mass. Afterward, he greeted the attendees, confirmed dinner invitations, and fielded prayer requests. By eight o'clock, the Blessed Sacrament was re-exposed and a silent rosary underway. At nine o'clock, the first of twenty-one eucharistic adorers would report, relieving Msgr. Steiner of his prayerful watch. The faithful adorers would cover one hour each until Msgr. Steiner reappeared in front of the Blessed Sacrament at six o'clock the following morning. Except for mass times, this perpetual adoration had occurred at St. Hubertus since 1973.

So, Cole knew exactly where to find Msgr. Steiner at 8:15 on a Monday morning: in his church, kneeling before the Blessed Sacrament, almost at the end of a rosary. Cole had not stepped foot in a church since the day that he walked out of the seminary three years prior. When he entered St. Hubertus that day, Cole was reminded of the beauty of old Catholic churches, even those small and rural. His eyes tracked to the Blessed Sacrament displayed in a monstrance that glowed, giving a warmth to the sanctuary. Cole did not genuflect, but took a seat in the pew across the aisle from Msgr. Steiner, and waited to be acknowledged.

Msgr. peeked at Cole, but finished his rosary. Then, he made the sign of the cross, got off his knees, and sat in the pew. He asked, "Why are you here?"

"I came back to see if I could help Jen with the boys, now that Boone is locked up."

"The last thing my niece needs is the kind of help you are here to give her, but what I meant is why you are here, in my church?"

"I wanted to see if you would help her get an annulment."

"I don't believe that is why you are here. She doesn't need my help to get an annulment and you know that. She married a non-Catholic, outside the church, as a teenager, and under duress. Rather, I think you're here for my blessing to marry her." Cole was too slow formulating a response, so Msgr. continued. "You have my blessing for three things and nothing more. You can confess your sins, do penance, and amend your life."

Cole stood, stepped into the aisle, and genuflected. Then, on his way out of church, he crossed himself with holy water.

A couple days later, Cole received an email from Msgr. Steiner asking him to come to the rectory the next time he was in the area. Optimistic that Msgr. had reconsidered and would give his blessing, Cole went to the rectory that evening. Msgr. saw him coming and opened the door for him. They went to the kitchen and Msgr. poured two glasses of homemade whiskey, made from the Steiner family recipe. Msgr. drained his glass, washing down a fistful of pills. Cole sipped his as Msgr. started to talk. "I'm sorry that I was so harsh before. I did not intend to demean your relationship with Jen. I know you love each other and your intentions are good."

"Thanks. I appreciate that."

Msgr. held up a finger and went on, "But you still can't have my blessing."

"What? Why not? You just said that we love each other."

"Love has nothing to do with it. People come to me all the time wanting permission to be with the one they love. When I can't indulge them, they cite fairness or extenuating circumstances. A sexual relationship is not the reward for loving someone. It is an act, both unitive and procreative, within the confines of sacramental marriage."

"But if she gets an annulment, there is no religious impediment to us marrying."

"That's correct, but your relationship would be harmful to the children."

"How?"

Msgr. explained, "It is good for you to step in for your brother and help raise your nephews, but it would scandalize those boys if their mother shared a bed with their uncle. They need their uncle in their life regardless of whether things are going well between you and their mother. In the past, when she hurt your feelings, you had nothing to do with them."

"That was the past. I'm committed, now, to being there for them, and Jen."

"And even if things go well, like you propose, at some point they will grow older and learn how the world works. They'll remember the circumstances of you magically appearing in their lives, and they will question your true motive in all that ever you did for them. You're free to put a millstone around your neck, but I'm not willing to join you. And being a celibate, I'm well acquainted with the fleshly sacrifice I'm asking of you. You were willing to sacrifice your body, maybe even your life, for your country, but not for the innocence of your nephews?"

Cole was in shock at this answer, "I honestly don't know how to respond to that, Msgr."

"I know it will be difficult for you, but for her sake and that of her boys, you need to let this go. Look to St. Joseph for guidance. He took Mary into his home and raised Jesus as his own, honorably forgoing connubial affections."

"I'm not Joseph."

"But you should strive to be like him." After a long silence, Msgr. asked, "Would you like me to hear your confession?"

"No, thanks." Cole felt only bitterness.

"Well then, come, sit, and watch the Cardinals game with me."

"I really have to get back to Jefferson City."

Msgr. let himself go soft. He missed Cole. "I'm old and my health is failing. Just stay with me until I fall asleep in this chair. It won't take long now that I've had my pills."

Cole's heart wrenched hearing Msgr. Steiner sound so vulnerable. "Okay, Msgr., I will."

Msgr. reclined the chair and was asleep before the inning was over. Cole let himself out and headed back to Jefferson City.

XXXIV.

Sister Paul Joseph was waiting for Jen when she reported to work the next morning. "Msgr. requested your presence in the church at 8:15. I'll fill in for you here while you're over there."

"Okay, thanks. Did he say why?"

"I think you know why," said Sister with a curt nod at the door, urging Jen to go.

Jen did suspect what the topic of the discussion would be, but she had no idea what he would say. She arrived at 8:15, took a seat and waited for Msgr. to finish his rosary. When he finished, Msgr. said, "Why is Cole asking for my blessing of your relationship?"

"We've been seeing each other."

Msgr. snarled, "Of course you're seeing each other and have been for a while. I'm neither blind nor a fool. But I asked why he is asking for my blessing to do so at this point." Msgr. regretted his outburst in front of the Blessed Sacrament and sought to calm himself before he spoke again.

"I told him that we couldn't get married unless we had your blessing."

Still irritated, but speaking less excitedly now, Msgr. asked, "But why? There's no impediment to your marriage. You don't need me to be involved."

"I know."

"And surely you knew that you would not get my blessing, considering the circumstances."

"I did."

"Then I'm forced to conclude that you sent him to me to end the relationship for you?"

Ashamed, Jen admitted, "I never thought we'd get to this point, but you were my safety net in case we did."

After a brief pause, Msgr. inquired in a kind and fatherly voice, "Why have you led him on?"

"The boys need someone like him in their lives. And I need someone like him in mine too. I tried, but I just can't fully commit to him in that way."

"Perhaps, it's because you know it's unhealthy for your boys."

"I swear, Uncle Gus, for all they know, he was just hanging out with them as their uncle."

He then directed Jen sternly, "You need to tell him the truth."

"I know."

"And not use me as the scapegoat."

"I know, I'm sorry for that."

Hoping the conversation was over, Jen stood to leave, but Msgr. was not finished. "Would you like me to hear your confession?"

"Not right now."

XXXV.

Jen invited Cole to her place the following night to tell him the truth. Cole noticed the peace and quiet in the trailer, and Jen explained, "The boys are spending the night at the Big House."

"That's good because I need to talk to you."

"I need to talk to you too."

Cole said, "Can I go first?" Jen nodded, and he proceeded with a rehearsed statement. "Because I wanted to be with you so much, I failed to appreciate the harm that our relationship might do to the boys. I will always be there for you all, but for you as a brother and for the boys as an uncle."

Happy disbelief flooded her, "Are you breaking up with me?"

"Yes."

"I love you."

"I know that this is hard, but with time, I think you'll agree it's the right thing to do."

"I didn't say I love you to change your mind. I said I love you because this is the nicest thing anyone has ever done for me."

"Breaking up with you is nice?" Cole looked confused.

"Since you're willing to give this up for my family, yes. I've known for a while that this wasn't going to work. It would have been too weird for me to marry the boys' uncle, but I led you around with a carrot on a stick anyway."

"You didn't lead me anywhere. I wanted to be in your lives."

"Cole, I'm really sorry that I wasn't honest with you. You have always deserved better than what I could give you." After an awkward pause, Jen said, "We could start tomorrow."

"Start what?"

"The break up." Jen looked to the rear of the trailer, at its only actual bedroom. "You could spend the night with me?" Before Cole could answer, Jen took his hand and led him where she already knew he wanted to go. Nearing the bedroom though, Cole stopped so abruptly that their hands separated. Jen turned to find Cole looking at an alcove with a set of bunkbeds, and beyond, a window sill decorated with trinkets that had once belonged to his mother.

As she watched him look at her boys' beds, Jen felt growing shame. She had only ever used her sexuality as a tool, to control Cole and to keep to Boone interested in supporting her. With this offer though, Jen had hoped, for the first time in her life, to simultaneously share both a physical and emotional connection with a man. She tried to rationalize this to herself as romantic, mutual support and comfort, or even a just reward for their friendship. But as she considered Cole's wariness, she realized that without further commitment, this act would be no different than the others.

"I'm so sorry. I shouldn't have done this." Jen's voice was quiet and trembled a bit. "Now I'm embarrassed."

"Don't say that. We have a long and complicated history. It's not like we just met on the internet."

"Still though," guilt and shame flooded her, and she didn't know what to say to make it go away.

Cole tried to mollify her, "You know I want to, but I can't." Jen smiled in agreement, and Cole added, "But I should leave before I change my mind." Somehow this relieved the tension and restored their old camaraderie.

On his way out, Jen said, "Cole?" He stopped to look at her, and she admitted, "I've never once told a man, other than you, that I loved him."

XXXVI.

Jen didn't sleep. In the morning, before she got the boys from the Big House, she stopped by the Christmas trees, knowing she'd find Msgr. with them on a Saturday morning. "Uncle Gus…, I hope some of these get picked next year as much effort as you put in them."

"I feel like I owe it to them. To give them every opportunity to not become mulch."

Jen looked at the trees, then back at her uncle, and said, "I talked to Cole last night."

"And?"

"I apologized for leading him on."

Msgr. asked, "How did he take it?"

"He actually broke up with me first. He said that our relationship could be bad for the boys."

"How do you feel about that?"

Jen thought about her answer. "I don't know. I just feel bad about how things worked out with him, like I robbed him of a happy life."

"How are you to blame for his life choices?"

"When we were in high school, before Boone, he begged to be together and I always said no."

"That was your prerogative." Msgr. sounded unmoved by Jen's admission.

Then, Jen began to cry. Msgr. walked Jen over to the tailgate of his truck and sat her down. He grabbed his stole from the cab, put it on, and sat next to her. Msgr. made the sign of the cross.

Through her tears, Jen confessed, "I refused him, so I could control him."

Msgr. nodded, welcoming Jen to continue.

Still crying, Jen admitted, "It didn't work, and then in my pride, I couldn't stand that he chose the seminary over me. Even though I wouldn't date him, I didn't want him moving on either. I wanted him here with me, following me around like a puppy." Jen paused to choose her words carefully, then confessed, "I was mad at him, and sad and lonely, and I slept with his brother."

Msgr. cringed hearing these words from his niece, but she had needed to say it out loud. "That was cruel. What else?"

"I committed adultery, I had sex with my husband's brother. I seduced Cole. I wanted to know if I still had power over him, and he left the seminary over it. I cost the church a priest because of my pride."

"Go on."

"Greed. I use the people I love. I go to church, so you and Sister Paul Joseph will keep helping me."

"What else?"

"Dishonesty. I let Cole think that we could be married even though I knew it would never happen."

"Is there anything else?"

Jen paused and became tearful once more. "Lust, last night…". Msgr. winced and braced himself, grabbing the side of his truck. "I offered my body to Cole. He turned me down, but I was willing." Jen, now sobbing, could not go on, so Msgr. took over.

"You're upset because your sins are terrible. Shortly, I will absolve you of them, so dwell on them no longer. The devil, the Liar, wants you to believe that you are no better than your sins. He fears that you will discover the truth, that you are a beloved child of God and that God is merciful and loves you unconditionally. Do your penance, which is one rosary for an increase in priestly vocations. Lastly, amend your life by drawing closer to God. Ask him in prayer for the strength to overcome future temptations. Now, make your act of contrition."

XXXVII.

Jimmy's disposition failed to improve with the sale of the business, and Lillian was exasperated by his incessant moping. At least when he was working, she had a break from his brooding, but now he was essentially retired, and Jimmy had few external distractions from his melancholy. Lillian wanted to give Jimmy an ultimatum, but she knew in her heart that she would never end the marriage. Even before they were bound by children and religious covenant, Lillian had a devotion to Jimmy that he had exploited. But even though Lillian expected her efforts to be in vain, she persisted in her ongoing struggle to fix the man she adored.

Christmas had always been the most difficult time of year for Jimmy, and while it would have been understandable for Lillian to dread it too, she didn't. Each year, she did the most with what they had to make Christmas special for her family. This year, their oldest, Gemma, still believed in Santa Claus, and their third, Benedict, was just old enough to understand. Only their newborn, Mary Regina, wouldn't be excited by it. So, Lillian had been looking forward to the children opening gifts. But on Christmas morning, Jimmy balked at participating. She coaxed him into the room, hoping that his spirits would be raised by the happiness of the children. With each gift though, Jimmy rolled his eyes or made a comment of disapproval.

When the children finished, Lillian sent them to the basement to play with their new toys. She turned to Jimmy and asked, "What is the matter with you?"

"You know that I hate the commercialism of Christmas and you spent more than ever this year."

"That's because we have more than ever. But I don't just mean this morning. I want to know why you can't enjoy anything, why you can't let me enjoy anything, and most importantly, why you insist on poisoning our children with your resentments? Actually, I'd like to know what you even have to be resentful about anymore. You've always found something to fuel your despondency. First, you didn't want to go to law school. Then, you didn't want a good paying job at a firm, but you didn't make enough money in your practice, or the work wasn't interesting enough. But now, what is it? You have beautiful and healthy children and a wife willing to endure almost all of your nonsense. You have enough money to do whatever you want or even nothing at all, but you're willing to squander it all. Why?"

Answerless, Jimmy just stared away from Lillian.

"I'm taking the kids to mass and then to my parents'. You're not welcome to join us.

You've already ruined Christmas for enough people and I won't subject the rest of my family to your moody outbursts. We'll spend the night there, maybe several. I just don't know anymore."

XXXVIII.

Jimmy spent the rest of Christmas day alone. For the most part, he sulked, blaming Lillian for not accepting him for who he had always been. The silence of the house began to haunt him though, and by nightfall he dreaded the prospect of losing his wife and children. Overnight, he resolved to make a change, but he didn't know how.

In the morning, Jimmy thought about his mother and how she had struggled to raise him alone. Then, he remembered that he had told Boone's wife he could help her, but realized he never actually did. Jimmy needed to make amends.

Jimmy drove to St. Hubertus and parked outside the gate of Steiner Farm. Walking past the field of Christmas trees, he heard a man's voice. "I guess you found Boone."

Turning toward the source of the voice, Jimmy recognized the man from his previous visit, dressed in a cassock this time, pruning lopper in hand. "I found him."

"I know. I watch the news."

Noticing the man's attire, Jimmy asked, "You're a priest?"

"Ordained to the Order of Melchizedek, are you Catholic?"

"From the cradle, but not so much anymore."

"What do you mean by that?

"I go through the motions, mostly to appease my wife, and for the sake of the children."

"So, you're a nonbeliever?"

After considering his answer, Jimmy responded, "That's correct."

"Then why go through the motions for the sake of the children?"

Caught off guard, Jimmy said, "Huh?"

"If there is nothing for you to believe, then there's nothing for the children to believe, right?"

Jimmy replied, "I want them to have faith."

"Why though?"

Jimmy looked away. He didn't seem to have an answer, so the priest continued, "Might it be that you do indeed believe? That you hope for the salvation of your children, but consider yourself irredcemable?"

Again, Jimmy remained silent.

"When was the last time you confessed your sins to a priest?"

Jimmy sniffed, "Second grade, my first, and only, reconciliation."

"Not even when you got married?"

Chuckling uncomfortably, Jimmy replied, "My wife, then fiancé, saw to it that there was nothing to confess."

"There's always something. Would you like me to hear your confession?"

"Father, I really appreciate this conversation, but I'm not prepared for that today."

"It doesn't have to be today." Gesturing towards the church, the priest continued, "I'm available to hear your confession at all hours of the day and night. Please come see me when you're ready."

Jimmy looked towards the stone church building, and then back at the priest. "Thank you, Father, I'll think about it. Merry Christmas." He left Msgr. to tend his Christmas trees and headed to the trailer.

As Jimmy neared the trailer, Jen opened the door and stepped onto the porch. "I thought the only way I'd see you again would be on T.V., but here you are."

"I have something for you."

"Is it child support, because that would be nice?"

"It could be, or you could spend it on yourself." Jimmy handed Jen a check for $10,000.

"Is this from Boone?"

"No, it's from me." Jimmy could sense that Jen's back went up. After all, some lawyer from St. Louis who she hardly knew was handing her check near the amount of her annual salary. So, Jimmy made up a reason to take the money she could accept. "It's a referral fee, for getting me in touch with Boone. It's standard practice, but if you don't want it, I'll take it back."

"No, I'll keep it. I'm just kind of shocked."

When Jimmy got back to his SUV, he realized that it was the first time in his adult life he was pleased by a Christmas gift, either given or received.

Lillian and the kids were waiting for him at home. He hugged the three oldest children and told them that he had missed them. Then, he picked up Mary Regina, turned to Lillian, and said, "I'm sorry for taking advantage of your loyalty. I won't do it again."

XXXIX.

Except for Sister Paul Joseph, the entire congregation was surprised to see Fr. Bob and not Msgr. Steiner say Sunday mass at St. Hubertus. Despite Fr. Bob's near proximity, Msgr. Steiner always looked elsewhere for a priest to cover his masses when he needed a substitute. But this time, it was the Bishop and not Msgr. Steiner who called on Fr. Bob to assist. During the announcements, Fr. Bob read the letter from Msgr. Steiner explaining the situation.

My spiritual children:

My doctor recently informed me that my condition is terminal. To her, I replied that my condition became terminal at the moment of conception. I thank God for this wonderful blessing though. With notice of my imminent departure, God afforded me the opportunity to confess my sins and do penance in preparation for my judgment. My beloved brother Gerhard, who some of you remember, did not have this opportunity. His death was sudden and untimely. I have prayed daily for over fifty-five years that Gerry glorified God's magnanimity and mercy.

I hope to soon have the honor of roasting in purgatory. In your charity, please pray, fast, give alms, and offer in my favor the holy sacrifice of the mass that I will not suffer too long for want of the beatific vision. I have an additional request to any who wish to further honor my memory. Before it is too late, confess your sins, do penance, and amend your life.

In Christ, Msgr.

XL.

Jen called Cole with the news right after mass. Cole had dreaded this day, knowing that it would come. He reflected on everything that Msgr. had done for him. Msgr. Steiner taught Cole justice and mercy by loving him in the stern, but unconditional, way that a father loves a son. Between Cole and Msgr. Steiner, "Father" was not just an earned title, but a relationship.

Cole was ashamed of himself, knowing that for years, he had been taking from Msgr. Steiner, never offering anything in return. He visited Msgr. that same day. A nurse met Cole at the rectory door and showed him to Msgr.'s hospital bed, in what once served as the living room. Cole couldn't believe how quickly Msgr.'s health had deteriorated. When Cole last saw Msgr., he looked merely worn. But now, only three months later, Msgr. was bedfast and struggled to speak.

With a frail voice, Msgr. introduced Cole to the nurse. "This is the son I've told you about."

"Is that true?" It was clear the nurse was fond of Msgr., but incredulous.

"Yes, it is," said Cole.

The nurse smiled, "I thought that he was just telling stories, you know, since he's a priest."

"Adopted son, but he is my father."

At that, Msgr. managed a smile, and when the nurse left, wasted no time on small talk. "Thank-you for the way you handled things with Jen. I know that wasn't easy for you."

"You were right."

"You're a good boy, and would have been a good husband to her if the circumstances were different." Still smarting from the break-up, Cole didn't respond, wanting to change the subject. Msgr. obliged, but chose an even more unpleasant topic. "I have two things to ask of you."

"You want to hear my confession?"

"I don't need to hear it, I just want to know it will happen."

Cole didn't commit, but asked, "What's your other request?"

"Pick up the broken pieces after I'm gone."

Cole tried to swallow the lump in his throat before answering, "Okay, Msgr., I'll do both."

Msgr. fell asleep and the nurse showed Cole to the door.

Msgr. passed during the night. Cole had never before considered the absolute mortality of priests. Without children, they leave no genetic footprint on earth. They have no descendants to pray for their souls and to offer masses on their behalf. They are just gone, some to an eternal reward.

XLI.

Msgr. Steiner's funeral mass was at the cathedral in Jefferson City. With Bishop Patrick Eagan officiating, all able priests of the diocese attended. At the request of Sister Paul Joseph, Cole served as a pallbearer, along with Uncle Pius, a man who introduced himself as Henry Steiner, and three Knights of Columbus from the St. Hubertus Council.

Msgr. would be buried in the St. Hubertus cemetery, but not until the ground thawed in spring. So, following the funeral mass, the mourners were invited to a gathering at the Big House on Steiner Farm, but the Bishop asked for a moment alone with Cole first. He asked, "You were a seminarian, right?"

"That's correct, Bishop."

"Do you feel comfortable sharing with me your reason for leaving?"

"I just lost faith, sir."

"Are you a believer?"

"Not anymore."

"In my experience, non-believers go to communion, following the herd, thinking nothing of it. I suspect that many of the attendees today received the Eucharist unworthily. I find it curious that you abstained though. For if the Eucharist was not indeed the body of Christ, there could be no harm in receiving it in any spiritual condition, right?"

Cole was speechless, so the Bishop finished his point.

"Just consider that perhaps you have not lost faith. I'd love to help you find your way back into the Church, and I want you to know that I have selfish reasons. I want you back in the seminary. You made quite the impression on your instructors there, and I'm in need of good priests."

"Bishop, I'm sorry, but I don't see the priesthood in my future."

"If something changes, or you just want some spiritual guidance, please contact me."

At the Big House, Cole spoke with Grandma Steiner for the first time in almost a decade. He knelt to greet her, so Grandma wouldn't have to get up from her chair, and she pulled him even closer to kiss both of his cheeks. While she looked him over, Cole said, "I'm sorry for your loss, Grandma."

She said, "It's unnatural for a parent to bury a child, and this is my third time."

Cole remembered that in addition to Gerhard, Msgr. had had a sister, Helen, who succumbed to illness. There was a picture of Helen with her three small children in the Big House, but it was outdated. Their father had remarried and moved the children out of state, severing relations with the Steiner family.

"It is nice to have all of my surviving children together for the first time since the last time I buried a child." Grandma chuckled to herself declaring, "The next time they'll be together will probably be for my funeral." Grandma then waved over her daughter Katherine. "Where's Mike?"

"Mother, we've been divorced almost thirty years."

"I know that, but he went to school with Augustine. He should have been here." Answerless, Katherine shrugged and walked away. Grandma leaned closer to Cole as if she would whisper, but instead spoke in a normal voice. "I still don't understand why she insisted on getting divorced. He wasn't any worse than other husbands."

Uncomfortable, both from kneeling and the topics of conversation, Cole stood to begin the process of excusing himself, but Grandma insisted that he sit with her, and ordered her son, Heinrich, to bring Cole a chair. Cole recognized Heinrich as the fellow pall bearer who went by Henry. "Oh…, Henry is Heinrich."

Grandma corrected Cole. "No, Heinrich is Heinrich, like my father."

Cole had always known Grandma to be persnickety about names and heritage, but she seemed even more fussy about Heinrich, so Cole said, "I'm sorry Grandma. I know how much names mean to you."

Grandma explained, "He's my last surviving son and there will be no more Steiners of St. Hubertus unless he produces a male heir." Then, pointing across the room at a man not familiar to Cole, Grandma said, "That's his roommate, Marco," but she looked skeptical. "I know they're more than friends, but I won't acknowledge it, at least until he finds the courage to tell me so."

Cole was uneasy, but Grandma wasn't finished venting, "It's immoral too, but no more so than Elizabeth living with Bill, and actually less so than Paula gallivanting from one man to the next." Grandma paused for a moment, then said, "So, when Heinrich is ready to say it, I'll acknowledge it."

When Cole saw Jen approaching, he stood to greet her. She seemed upset, not quite crying, but shook. Without speaking, she gave him a hug. She nudged Cole, so they could speak in private, and only a few steps away, Jen was frantic. "She's moving back. She wants to live with us. There's no room as it is, and even if there was, I can't deal with her shit. I have four boys to raise, I can't coddle my mother too."

XLII.

Sister Paul Joseph overheard Jen's conversation with Cole and was furious with her sister. She went outside to cool off in the winter air and to consider the situation. Over the decades, she and Msgr. had dozens of times assisted family, parishioners, and others through difficult times. They rarely agreed on the best course of action, but through compromise, almost always found a solution to best help those in need. This time though, she would have to do it on her own. She would have never admitted it while he was alive, but she missed her brother's wise counsel.

With her plan made, Sister Paul Joseph marched back into the Big House. She found Paula, grabbed her by the arm, and escorted her out of the house. Alone on the front porch, Sister Paul Joseph pointed her finger and admonished her younger sister. "You're not moving back to this farm."

Paula pushed back. "My daughter and grandsons need me."

"Your daughter needed a mother and your grandsons needed a grandmother, but they don't need you."

Paula then played her trump card. "It's my trailer, maybe I'll move it off the farm and live in it. Of course, Jen and the boys are welcome to join me."

Sister Paul Joseph glared at Paula, then asked, "How much?" Paula didn't answer right away, so Sister Paul Joseph clarified. "How much do you want for your trailer?"

"$12,000."

"Wait here." Sister Paul Joseph went into the house, and when she returned a couple minutes later, handed Paula a check for $5,000. Paula didn't haggle. Instead, she said goodbye to her mother, Jen, and the boys, and left Steiner Farm for good.

XLIII.

Cole kept his word to Jen, doing the things that uncles do for nephews as well as the things that brothers do for sisters. He faded into the background when Boone was released from prison. Since the State of Missouri insisted on Boone paying child support, he wanted to "get something for his money," so he came around from time to time, visiting the boys at the trailer. This arrangement suited Jen better than the alternative. She would rather Boone "make a nuisance of himself" at her place than to take the boys off to his new family, where she could not supervise.

While Cole was glad for the boys that their father did not abandon them, he had no interest in seeing his brother. But when it was time for Hunter's First Communion Cole told Jen he would come, even after she warned him that Hunter had invited Boone.

"That's fine," said Cole.

"I don't think he'll come to church, but he says he's coming to the party. Who knows though. It's Boone, so you never know."

Cole didn't know why, but he was unwilling to miss Hunter's First Communion. "I'll be at both."

When Cole arrived at the church, Sister Paul Joseph waved for him to join them in the Steiner family pew. She'd always kept Cole at arm's length, even when he had a great relationship with Msgr. Steiner. Cole had always assumed that she either didn't like him or didn't trust him, but something had changed. Cole was also surprised by the lack of people in the church with mass about to start. For First Communions, church was always packed with extended family. Cole asked Jen if she knew why.

"There's only six kids in Hunter's class now."

"What? I remember class sizes being like fifteen, at least."

"Actually, yes, just a couple years ago."

"What happened?"

"Fr. Bob started charging tuition. Msgr. let all active parishioners send their kids for free, using the tithes of all parishioners to fund the school. With the change, a lot of parents couldn't afford the tuition and pulled their kids. It's so bad now that two grades share a classroom and teacher. Thankfully, the boys get free tuition since I work here, or I wouldn't be able to afford it either." Cole shook his head in disappointment. "Sister has not said much to me, but I don't see how the school can stay open much longer."

As they sat through the mass, Cole became more and more discomforted. He identified more than a dozen liturgical abuses. He had not concerned himself with church matters in years, but still, he knew this mass was an abomination. Cole was incredulous at how fast this parish had declined. For over forty years, Msgr. had tended his flock, but now most of the flock was scattered and the remainder without a true shepherd.

On his way to the party, Cole noticed Msgr.'s Christmas trees. The field was no longer kept. Thick weeds and high grass filled the spaces between the trees and vines choked the branches.

Boone came to the party, but Cole ignored him for as long as possible. Cole was throwing a football with Bo in the yard when Boone came out and told Bo to get him a beer. Left alone, the brothers exchanged words for the first time in a decade.

"Thanks for looking after things while I was away." At first, Cole was surprised that his brother was so gracious, but Boone wasn't finished. "Are you screwing her?"

"What? No."

"It's okay with me if you do, I've had my fill of it." Boone took a long drag from his cigarette, and asked, "What? Are you too good for your brother's table scraps?"

"No, she's too good for either of us."

Boone made a show of looking around taking a head count of his sons with Jen. "That's not how I see it. Anyway, if you want to have a turn with her, go ahead. She's easy, so it won't be too hard, even for you."

Cole knew exactly what Boone wanted from the exchange. As children, Boone would beat up his younger brother as a hobby, but things would be different now. Boone was emaciated from prison nutrition and his muscles atrophied from a lifetime of drug use. Cole, on the other hand, was muscular, not like a body builder, but a middle-distance runner. Cole had fantasized about serving revenge to his brother in the form of a beating, and the only people at that party who would have objected to him doing so were the boys. Cole could not bear to upset them though. He also remembered Msgr.'s rule to "kill your enemies with kindness," but Cole could not muster any, so he just suffered Boone in peace. When Bo returned with the beer, Boone took it and walked away.

Since Gerhard II's death, Uncle Pius farmed all the Steiner land, except the field of Christmas trees. So, Cole knew that any concerns regarding Steiner Farm should be addressed to him. So, later at the party, Cole approached Pius, who was married to Jen's Aunt Josephine. Josephine was barren, which irritated Grandma Steiner. Cole remembered Grandma once saying that she knew infertility "was a real thing because it's in the Bible," but blamed Pius as "not ambitious enough to get her pregnant."

Uncle Pius was a good-natured man, but so quiet that folks just left him alone at social functions. He did not seem to mind this. He would speak when spoken to, but minimally. Hoping to start a conversation that would lead naturally towards his point, Cole noted, "The Christmas trees are overgrown with weeds," but Uncle Pius simply nodded in agreement. So, Cole had to ask point blank, "Is there anything that can be done to maintain the field better?"

Uncle Pius replied, "It could be mowed." Cole hoped that Uncle Pius would volunteer his services or equipment for the project, but Uncle Pius did not take the hint. With the conversation going nowhere, Cole found Sister Paul Joseph, who was the trustee of Steiner Farm.

"What can I do to help maintain the Christmas trees?"

"You're willing to do that?" She sounded surprised.

"Yes, I can't stand to see the field look like that."

"It definitely needs to be mowed and the vines cut back, and the weeds should be sprayed too. I'll have Pius bring the riding mower and some equipment to the cabin for you."

"Thanks."

"No Cole, thank you."

XLIV.

Cole realized his blunder in stopping by so early on a Saturday morning when Jen opened the trailer door with only one eye open and still in her pajamas. "Oh, sorry."

"It's okay, I've been up for hours, churning butter."

Cole got her point. "Alright. I should have let you know I was coming, but I didn't think that far ahead."

"Well? Why are you here?"

"I came to clean up the Christmas tree field and I thought the boys may want to help or just keep me company." Cole heard yelps of excitement and some bustle and looked past Jen to see half-dressed boys scurrying around the trailer, throwing on jeans and boots.

Jen looked at them and then back at Cole, "It looks like it's a yes from them."

Archer only lasted thirty minutes at the field before Cole had to stop and take him back to Jen, but Bo, Hunter, and Shooter helped all morning. Cole even let them take turns driving the mower. The field was much improved after just that one morning of work, but still needed regular attention, and Cole returned each week, for a while, to care for the trees.

Jen asked Cole to stay for lunch, and he did. He thought she may have regretted the invitation though when the boys started asking questions.

Hunter asked, "Why don't you always go to church with us, like you did for my First Communion?"

Bo answered on Cole's behalf, "Because his church is in Jefferson City, where he lives."

Cole corrected Bo, "I actually don't go to church unless it's an important occasion for you guys."

Bo and Hunter then asked, almost at the same time, "Why not?"

Jen interrupted, "That's none of your business. You two are a couple of Nosy Rosies."

Cole felt a duty to be forthright with his nephews, and he didn't want to glorify his disconnection from the faith. "I am too embarrassed of my sins to tell a priest, so I can't go to communion, and when I am in church, I'm reminded that I am separated from Jesus only because of my pride."

But Shooter responded, "You should still go to church."

XLV.

Cole continued to have his dreams about the woman in Iraq but after Msgr.'s death, they changed. While the dreams started like before, with Cole in his Army uniform driving a Humvee, he was now fleeing a deer instead of an IED attack. He would drive faster, becoming desperate to get away from the deer. Not able to drive fast enough, he would turn into a field of Christmas trees, mowing them down. This would continue until he'd hit the Iraqi woman. He'd get out of the vehicle to help her, and when he'd removed her head scarf, it was always Jen. He would try, but could not help her. He would then back away from her and observe his surroundings, a destroyed field of Christmas trees and a deer leering at him from a distance.

He had the dream almost every night now. It did not terrorize him. He never awoke in fear or panic, but instead would be wired and unable to sleep for the rest of the night. After months of chronic sleep deprivation, Cole decided to stop running from the deer, and like Hubertus, he presented himself to his bishop for spiritual direction.

Bishop Eagan was a busy man, but made time in the hope of getting a new priest. Cole did not have to wait long in the reception area of the chancery before the Bishop appeared, welcomed him, and showed him back to his office. "I'm glad you came. How can I help you?"

"I promised Msgr. Steiner that I would make a good confession, and I want you to hear it."

"I'm happy to do so, but why come all this way for that?"

"Because after you hear what I have to say, you can tell me whether you would even want me as a priest in your diocese."

The Bishop produced a stole from his desk drawer and made the sign of the cross.

"Bless me Bishop for I have sinned, it has been four years since my last confession."

"What are your sins?"

"Pride…, I forsook my nephews because their mother and father hurt me. I defied the church and her rules because I was too prideful to confess my sins. I was away from the Church for years. I dishonored my father…"

"How so?"

"I went to war and returned and never let him know that I was okay and home safely until I needed something from him."

"Good, go on."

"I made an idol of a woman. I worshipped her. I put her before God."

"Definitely sinful, but a natural flaw for a man."

"This woman, my brother's wife, I coveted her."

"That tends to go along with the worship, but sinful nonetheless."

"I had sex with her."

"And then you left the seminary?"

"Yes, Bishop."

"Anything else?"

"Probably, but these are all of the mortal sins that I can recall at this time."

"Very good then. Your recitation was refreshingly honest. Bishops are often presented a gilded version of their flock. I sometimes get a complex thinking that my sheep are holier than I am, but it's all a veneer. I suspect that the sin you believe disqualifies you from the priesthood is this business with the woman."

"Well most of the sins I mentioned do involve her in some way."

"Yes, but it's the sexual sin that you are hung up on, isn't it?"

"I suppose, yes, Bishop."

"How many times?"

"Once."

"How many times did you miss Sunday or holy day mass in this time?

"I don't know, close to two hundred times, I guess."

"All of these are mortal sins in the eyes of God, but we tend to fixate on the sexual ones, don't we? I've never understood that, but it probably has something to do with Adam and Eve."

"You don't know?"

"I'm a Bishop, not a theologian. The Holy Father needs me to administer a diocese, not know these things. Likewise, I don't need you to be Msgr. Steiner, I just need you to be Fr. Beck."

"But I'm not sure I'm ready to commit."

"And I'm not sure that I want you yet, but on his deathbed, Msgr. Steiner pressed me to pursue you. He bragged on your high moral character and your profound sense of duty, but after what I heard today, I have reservations."

Cole was somewhat disappointed and said, "Oh."

"And it's not because of your dalliance with the woman. That's among the most normal things a seminarian can confess. It's because I need to be sure that you will not turn back to her, in a moment of weakness or if circumstances change. Consider the institution of priestly celibacy. A benefit is that it keeps priests from having competing loyalties. A priest may not be available to race to the bedside of an ill parishioner if he has sick kids of his own. Or what if a priest faces martyrdom, it's much harder to accept that fate with a wife and children waiting at home. So, you must first subjugate any loyalty you have to this woman before I will consider you for ordination. For your penance, I want you to pray one rosary that the Holy Spirit will guide you in your discernment. Now make your Act of Contrition."

Cole did so, and the Bishop absolved him of his sins.

Cole drove straight to St. Hubertus. He wanted to do his penance in Msgr. Steiner's spot before the Blessed Sacrament. Cole thought that the eucharistic adorer for that hour would be glad for the company. But when Cole arrived just before sundown, the church door was locked, and the rectory was dark. Demoralized, Cole returned to his truck and prayed his rosary. His despair lifted though, as he admired his handiwork, the groomed field of Christmas trees, visible from his parking spot.

Before leaving town, Cole stopped by Jen's trailer. "I'm sorry for coming unannounced again."

Exasperated, and with kids running around behind her, Jen barked at him, "I was trying to put these fool children to bed and now they're stirred up again," then she relented and smiled, "but this is better than predawn, so come on in."

Jen set the ground rules for the visit. "You may tell Uncle Cole one story each and then you go back to bed. We'll go youngest to oldest. Now start." What should have lasted less than five minutes, took nearly forty, and Cole could tell that Jen was still irritated with him. So, when the last went to bed, he apologized again.

"Cole, it's fine."

Cole was pretty sure that it was not fine, but he was glad that she pretended anyway. "I went by the church and it was locked. I don't think it was locked for thirty-five years, with perpetual adoration."

"Oh…They stopped that."

"Fr. Bob?"

"They just didn't have enough people willing to be there all hours."

"So, Fr. Bob."

"I think he means well, but things have gone downhill. He does have two parishes now with us and St. Barnabas."

"I saw the rectory was closed up too."

"He's still lives over at St. Barnabas, and just comes here when he has to."

Cole grumbled to himself about the state of the parish before asking Jen, "How would you feel if I went back to seminary."

"I think I would react better than last time."

Cole joked at her, "Well I do only have one brother," but she responded with hurt and anger.

"Cole! You're a shit and that was mean."

"I'm sorry, I really didn't intend it to be mean, but if we can have this conversation, and make some jokes, then laugh, it's a good thing. Isn't it?"

Jen sulked for a moment and then admitted, "It was a little funny and I kind of deserved it."

"You didn't deserve Boone though."

"And neither did you." They sat regarding each other for a moment, and then nodded, reaching an unspoken agreement. Jen went on, "Cole, I want nothing more than for you to be happy, whether that's as a single uncle, or as a husband to another woman, or as a priest. I long ago forfeited any right to an opinion on your life."

At peace with Jen for perhaps the first time in his life, Cole returned to Jefferson City and packed for St. Louis and the seminary.

XLVI.

Just over a year later, Cole was ordained as a transitional deacon, and assigned to the Cathedral parish in Jefferson City to assist the pastor. The Cathedral's pastor, Msgr. La Conte, was glad to share a rectory with a fellow veteran and he kept the Bishop updated on Cole's performance. Then, after six months in this assignment, the Bishop summoned Cole to his office.

The Bishop didn't waste time on small talk. "I'd like you to stay here at the Cathedral with us a while longer."

"Yes, Bishop." Cole didn't question the Bishop, but had been hoping for some news regarding ordination.

"It's no secret in this diocese that liturgical precision isn't my strength, but you're orthodox and a rule follower, and I need someone like you as my master of ceremonies, to keep me out of trouble with my critics." Cole appreciated the compliment and smiled. "You'll also serve as Msgr. La Conte's associate pastor."

"Associate pastor?" Cole perked up.

"Oh. Sorry, I should've started by informing you that I set your ordination for June 19."

As his ordination approached, Cole considered how he would handle the various Catholic traditions. Cole chose St. Hubertus for his first mass, and planned to hear his first confessions there beforehand. But Cole would have no parents at his Ordination Mass, so he didn't know who he should give his manutergium and the first confessional stole to. So, Cole decided to keep them. In addition to the priests of the diocese, Jen, the boys, Sister Paul Joseph, the spinsters, Uncle Pius, and Aunt Josephine attended the ordination at the Cathedral. Grandma Steiner was unable to make the trip, but sent a gift with Sister Paul Joseph, the biretta that she and her husband gave their son Augustine the day of his ordination.

The following day, Fr. Beck heard his first confession. He was nervous leading up to it, and even more so when he heard the voice of Sister Paul Joseph. "Bless me father for I have sinned, it's been more than three years since my last confession." Sister Paul Joseph then proceeded with a litany of venial sins. In summary, she was temperamental and impatient. Fr. Beck had expected this type of confession from an older woman, but then she slowed down, and her voice trembled as she continued:

> "I was uncharitable to a young man. He was orphaned as a teenager. My brother was kind enough to care for him as a father would, but I pretended to not

notice him. He needed maternal love and guidance, and I denied him these. With no children of my own, it's my vocation to fill in as a mother would, but I failed this young man. I took the first opportunity I had to send him away. It's not an excuse, but I was trying to protect my niece, for whom I've acted as a mother at times. I feared that with the bad example set by her own mother, she would act impulsively with the young man, that she would have babies too young, and that she would languish in her mother's trailer, relying on the charity of others. I was vain to think that my actions would keep these things from happening, and I hope you'll forgive me."

Fr. Beck interrupted, uninterested in whether she had additional sins to confess. Her words, though touching, were still painful to hear, and he just wanted them to stop. "For your penance say three Hail Mary's. Now make your act of contrition." When she finished, Fr. Beck quickly, and without stopping for a breath, gave absolution.

After hearing confessions, Fr. Beck vested for his first mass. Then, he gathered Bo and Hunter, his servers for the mass, and they waited near the entrance for the music to start. Fr. Beck was focused on the mass, determined to not make any mistakes. During the penitential act though, Fr. Beck became distracted. When he said, "And to you, my brothers and sisters," Cole looked at Jen, and he remembered, as a teenager, volunteering to serve mass just for the view he'd have of her sitting in that same row. The memory was fond, but with "in what I have failed to do," Cole felt light-headed. He closed his eyes, trying to stay upright, but with "Amen," could no longer. He plopped in the Presider's chair and attempted to collect himself. When the music for the Gloria started, he stood again, and hoped the incident would be dismissed as simply the jitters of a new priest.

After mass, Fr. Beck greeted the attendees and accepted their well-wishes. Soon though, the church was empty. Fr. Bob had left keys and asked Fr. Beck to lock up on his way out, but he just wasn't ready to do that. He was nostalgic for Msgr. Steiner's St. Hubertus, the thriving parish where the doors were never locked. So, he found the monstrance in the sacristy and dusted it off. Then, he went to the tabernacle, chose a host, and displayed the monstrance on the altar, with the Blessed Sacrament exposed.

Fr. Beck prayed, kneeling in Msgr.'s spot for as long as he could. Then, he sat back in the pew and continued to pray until he heard the church doors open, then thunder to a close. Fr. Beck turned and saw Jen walking toward him.

She genuflected and took a seat next to him in the pew.

"Are you okay," she whispered. "I saw your truck still out there and thought I should check on you."

Fr. Beck nodded, then mentioned, "I didn't hear your confession today." He was being playful with his old friend.

"I wouldn't hold your breath waiting for it either. I'm not sure I can be that intimate with you. So, I'll keep going to Fr. Bob, if that's okay."

"That's fine with me." Fr. Beck smiled. "I don't want to hear it."

Jen reached over and squeezed Fr. Beck's hand just long enough to say, "I'm proud of you and I love you." Jen then stood, stepped into the aisle, and genuflected. She crossed herself with holy water on her way out of church and walked back to Steiner Farm.

XLVII.

Jen knew of Joseph Eldringhoff most of her life, but since he was nearly ten years her senior, she never actually met him until his girls came to the preschool class she assisted. The teacher, Mrs. Schneider, had prepared Jen for their arrival, making sure she was aware that their mother was deceased. It was the girls' first year in preschool and Mrs. Schneider anticipated them being out of sorts enough without having that topic come up.

When they arrived for their first day, Jen greeted the girls at the door. "Good morning, I'm Miss Jen. What are your names?"

The girls looked at their father, who to Jen resembled Shrek. He answered for them. "This is Gianna, and this is Chiara." Joseph patted each girl on her head as he said her name.

Jen was flummoxed by just how identical the twins looked, and asked, "How do you tell them apart?"

"I can't explain how to do it by looks, I just know. Their grandmothers can do it by personality and the foods they each like. Things like that are probably your best bet."

"Can I just call them both angel?"

Joseph smiled at Jen and said, "They might actually like that."

Joseph picked the girls up, one in each arm, and hugged them good bye. Back on the ground, the girls went to play with the other kids. Alone for the moment, Joseph asked, "Are you Msgr. Steiner's niece by any chance?"

"Yes, I am. What made you think that?"

"He told me once that he had a niece named Jen, and St. Hubertus is the Steiner family business, right?"

Jen laughed a little. "Whatever he said about me isn't true."

"So, you're not tough and resourceful?"

Jen blushed. "I'm sure he had more to say about me than that."

"He did, but that was the take away for me." Jen drew a breath and held it, trying to come up with a witty retort, but couldn't find one before Joseph changed the subject back to the girls. "They've never had to answer to anyone other than me and their grandmothers, so I hope they don't give you too much trouble."

By then, Jen recovered enough of her personality to quip, "Don't worry, I'll have them answering to a whistle like the von Trapp kids before you come back." Joseph didn't seem to understand the reference, so Jen clarified, "From the Sound of Music?"

"I don't watch much TV."

"It's a movie…actually a musical and a movie, but either way, you've never heard of it?"

"I've heard of it, I guess, but don't know anything about it."

Jen noticed that Mrs. Schneider was eager to get the school day underway, so she showed Joseph to the door. She said, "You should watch it. It's my favorite."

"Alright, I will."

Jen soon found herself looking forward to Joseph's arrival in the mornings and his return in the afternoons. She was enchanted by his old-fashioned and chivalrous ways, and as she saw more of him, she thought he looked less like Shrek and more like John Wayne.

Jen liked to mother Joseph's girls, and he noticed. One Friday, Joseph told Jen, "Thank you for fixing the girls' hair. They always look better when I pick them up than they did when I dropped them off."

Jen lied, "It's just part of the job."

Joseph then asked, "Will I see you tomorrow?"

At first, Jen wasn't sure what he meant, but then remembered it was the weekend of the annual parish fundraiser dinner and auction. "No, I'm sorry, but I won't be there."

"Oh? Would you like to go with me? The tickets come in pairs, and I'd rather have you as a date than eat two plates of food."

Jen had a physical, but pleasant reaction in her stomach hearing the word "date." "Look I would very much like to be your date, for this or even something else, but every person that I would consider leaving my boys with will be there too." She then started thinking aloud, "Well the oldest ones can fend for themselves, but the youngest, I'm just not sure I can leave him without adult supervision. Well, maybe it'll be okay…"

Joseph interrupted, "Please don't do anything that makes you uncomfortable. We can always have a date at a better time." Joseph gathered his girls and started for the door, but Jen stopped him.

"I might have another option. Can I call you tonight with my answer?"

"I don't intend to take anyone else, so you actually have until tomorrow evening to let me know."

"Thanks, but I'll let you know tonight."

XLVIII.

Fr. Beck was worried that something may be wrong when he saw that Jen was calling instead of texting. He answered, "Hello?"

"I have a big favor to ask you."

"You know I'll do it if I can."

"Can you watch the boys Saturday evening?"

"Well, I have the vigil mass, but if I can get Msgr. to switch with me, I'll do it. I don't expect him to object though."

"That would be great. Bo and Hunter, and even probably Shooter, are old enough to mostly take care of themselves, but I'm just not comfortable leaving Archer with them alone."

"That's fine, we'll just all hang out, they don't even need to know I'm there to watch them."

"There's something else you should know, I'm going to the St. Hubertus dinner and auction."

"Okay?"

"With a man…"

"So, a date?"

"Yes. Will that be too weird for you?"

Fr. Beck lied, "It's fine."

The next day, on his way to Jen's, Fr. Beck assessed the state of the Christmas trees. When away at seminary and now busy with priestly duties, he was unable to attend the trees. Sister

Paul Joseph had managed to motivate Uncle Pius just enough to mow between them from time to time. While that helped, Fr. Beck concluded that the trees needed more personalized care to thrive as they had under Msgr.'s watch.

    Jen was still getting ready when Fr. Beck arrived, so Bo opened the door for him. When Jen did emerge, she sent the boys outside, so they could speak alone. "They've already had dinner, but they'll try to eat every last snack in the place as soon as I leave. Frankly, I don't care if they do if that makes it easier for you."

    "We'll be fine, what about bedtimes?"

    "If you can make bedtime happen at all, awesome."

    Fr. Beck noticed her look. She was fashionable, yet modest, and he had the urge to compliment her, but decided to not complicate the situation. Instead, he asked, "Is your date picking you up?"

    "Yes, I wanted him to meet my boys."

    "How do you think they'll react?"

    "I'm not sure." She touched his shoulder. "I was including you when I said I wanted him to meet my boys."

    Before Fr. Beck could respond, they heard Joseph's truck approaching the trailer and Jen dashed outside, concerned about what the boys might say or ask if left alone with him. Fr. Beck followed Jen out, so everyone could be introduced.

Because of his size, Joseph was a distinctive man, and Fr. Beck remembered him, even though more than a dozen years had passed. When they shook hands, Fr. Beck felt like he had grabbed a cinder block, and he had an acute awareness that he was in the presence of a dominant rival. Joseph held the door for Jen and nodded at Fr. Beck as he got in his truck and they drove off, leaving the priest alone with his nephews for the evening.

To pass the time, Fr. Beck devised a series of simple competitions, like relay races and rock throwing for both distance and accuracy, and he even handicapped the games in favor of the younger boys. Fr. Beck was pleased by the sight of his nephews supporting and encouraging each other, even being gracious in defeat. At dusk, Fr. Beck called an end to the games and declared champions, ensuring that each boy won at least once. When they were all in the trailer for the evening, Fr. Beck had the boys get ready for bed, and asked Bo to help Archer.

Through the years, Fr. Beck had spent a lot of time in that trailer, but he had never internalized the living arrangement until that evening. The trailer was austere, with only one bathroom, a meagerly appointed living area, and a small galley kitchen that was ill-equipped to cook for a family. It had only one bedroom, crammed with a full-sized bed and a toddler bed. The only other sleeping area was an alcove with a set of twin-size bunkbeds. With only four beds in the trailer, Fr. Beck thought that Jen must still have Archer sleeping with her.

At ten o'clock, Fr. Beck fibbed, announcing it was bedtime per their mother's direction. Even the older boys obliged with only minimal debate. Hunter and Shooter took the bunkbeds, Archer climbed in the toddler bed, and Bo got in the full-sized bed.

Father Beck was surprised. "Is this how you guys usually sleep?" he asked Bo.

"Yes," Bo said, rubbing his eyes, "my mom usually just sleeps on the couch."

All four boys passed out quickly, and Fr. Beck spent the rest of the evening in prayer and reflection on the sacrifices that Jen made to provide for her family. The event ended at eleven, and even though he did not need to be back in Jefferson City before 7:30 mass in the morning, Fr. Beck was relieved to hear Joseph's truck at 11:05. Jen entered the trailer almost immediately, and Fr. Beck convinced himself that the farewell must have been uneventful.

Jen asked, "How was it?"

"They were great. No problems."

"I meant, how was it being here while I was out with another man?"

"Sometimes we do things that aren't particularly pleasant because they're the right things to do."

"That's the truth."

After a moment, Fr. Beck asked, "Do you ever think about how things would have been different if you could go back and…"

Jen interrupted, "What? Take a do-over?" Her tone conveyed unmistakable disinterest in his hypothetical. "I could've had one at the time with Bo, if I wanted to, but I didn't. So, I don't allow myself to think about it."

Fr. Beck knew exactly what Jen meant and his stomach turned. "I'm sorry, I didn't mean to…. It's just that I've spent a lot of time over the years thinking about how things could've been different, and tonight, I wanted to let you know…" Fr. Beck paused to choose his words carefully, "That I'm glad you didn't take the do-over."

Jen smiled, leaned over, and kissed Fr. Beck on the cheek. She then wiped the kiss with her hand, and observed, "You got farther with me tonight than my date did."

XLIX.

Jen saw Joseph a couple more times outside of school before he asked her to a matinee performance of the Sound of Music at the Fox Theatre in St. Louis. Early in the show, Jen could tell that Joseph was upset. His eyes, though tear free, were red and swollen. She whispered to herself, "Oh shit," when she realized that a musical about a widower raising children was perhaps not her best recommendation for a man in a similar situation. She didn't know what to do to make him feel better. They had not been physically intimate in any way, and she wasn't sure if she should touch him, but she didn't know what else to do. So, she put her hand on his shoulder, hoping that she had not been too forward.

On their way home, Joseph said, 'I'm sorry you had to see that. It wasn't polite for me to be out with you and thinking about her."

"You don't need to apologize."

"I'm still embarrassed you saw me like that. Not too many people have ever seen that side of me."

Jen wanted Joseph to feel better, so she said, "I'll tell you my embarrassing story about the Sound of Music. It'll be like kids doing the old 'I'll show you mine if you show me yours.'" Jen was also being intentionally suggestive, hoping to distract Joseph from his sorrow.

Joseph said, "Okay, what's the story."

Jen needed a moment to conjure some dark and distant moments. She took a deep breath then said, "We only had two TV channels when I was little, so our entertainment options were pretty limited. We did have a VCR and my mom taped the Sound of Music for me. She'd pop it in every time she had some guy over and didn't want me interrupting them."

Jen started breathing heavier and Joseph took his eyes off the road to see if she was okay. Then, she said, "The rest of this I've never told a living soul."

Joseph said, "You don't need to tell me."

"Yes, I think I do." Jen tried to slow her breathing, but she couldn't. "I never met my father, but when I was a little girl, my mom would tell me grand tales of their romance. By the time I was ten, I was suspicious of her stories because they weren't consistent. I decided that it was all bullshit, that she didn't even know who he was. I never called her on it though. I let her have her stories, but every time she put that movie on, I'd imagine that Captain von Trapp was my dad."

Jen paused, worried about what Joseph would think of her if she said more, but decided to tell him anyway. "But then I got a little older, and I what I wanted changed. I didn't think about the Captain being my dad, but the actor, Christopher Plummer, being my lover. When I was seventeen, I was lonely, and I thought I could make myself feel better. I just needed a guy. It didn't matter who, because he wasn't going to be Christopher Plummer anyway."

Jen wrinkled her face fighting through some tears. "I got pregnant, then married, and I spent the next eight years with my eyes closed pretending he was Christopher Plummer."

Now having revealed so much, Jen felt the need to explain. "There's a lot more I'm not proud of, but before this thing goes too far with us, I want you to know everything."

Joseph responded, "I don't need to know everything." He reached over and took her hand. "What you've done isn't who you are."

L.

Joseph invited Jen to have dinner at his house the following Saturday and she wasn't sure what to expect from the date. If Joseph was the man she thought he was, she would be home at a respectable hour. And while she wanted him to be that man, she also knew that if he was not, she'd welcome any advance that he would make. So, she sent the boys to stay overnight at the Big House, just in case.

After Jen got the boys situated at the Big House, Grandma stopped Jen on her way out and said, "What's this about you having dinner at Eldringhoff Farm?"

"What? How'd you know? I didn't tell anyone that."

"This isn't my first day in St. Hubertus, dear." Jen blushed as Grandma continued. "Joseph is a good man, like the ones we used to have around here."

Jen smiled and said, "I know Grandma, but thanks for saying so." Then she bent down to kiss Grandma on the cheek.

Jen had never been to Eldringhoff Farm, and when she arrived, remarked, "I can't believe how much your house looks like the Big House on Steiner Farm."

"That's because my grandfather, Eberhard Eldringhoff, and your grandfather, Gerhard Steiner, built them both together."

Jen thought she should've known that already. It's the type of thing that Grandma would have repeated, but it was nice to hear, coming from Joseph, that the connection between their families transcended generations. "Have you lived here your whole life?"

"Quite literally. I was born right over there." Joseph pointed to the kitchen floor. "When Maria and I married, my mom and dad moved to a small house in town."

Jen looked up the stairs. "Two bedrooms up there like the Big House?"

"That's right. The girls share a room in case I ever need one for boys."

Jen smiled, and Joseph excused himself to put their steaks on the grill. While he was outside, Jen took a closer look at some framed family photos in a curio cabinet. She found one from Joseph's wedding and sighed, then whispered "Christ, did she have to be beautiful too?"

When Joseph returned, they were ready to eat. The house had a dining room, but they ate instead at a small café table in kitchen. In addition to steak, they had creamed spinach and a roasted beet salad. Before sitting, Joseph uncorked a bottle of homemade wine and poured two glasses. When Joseph sat, Jen picked her fork up to eat, but Joseph bowed his head to pray. Hoping Joseph wouldn't notice,

Jen slid the fork back in its place and joined him in prayer.

On the steak, Jen noticed a symbol seared into the meat. She asked, "How'd you do that?"

"With a branding iron."

"Is it a butterfly?"

"No, but a lot of people guess that. I'll give you a hint." Joseph pointed to a large piece of iron in the same pattern on the wall above the mantle.

"A four-leaf clover?"

"No, it's our family brand, double rounded E's, facing one another, the initials of Eberhard Eldringhoff."

"Oh, I see that now. Do you still brand cattle?"

No, just steaks these days. We've used modern tagging techniques for as long as I can remember, but the farm still has a functioning forge, and I do some blacksmithing as a hobby."

After only a couple bites of food, Jen remarked "This is really good Joseph."

"Thanks. Almost everything we're eating came from this farm."

"Did you grow it all yourself?"

"No, I'm just a cattleman, but my uncle Frederick grew the vegetables and the herbs. His wife, Annette, even made the wine and the vinegar from Norton grapes they grow here. They live just down the road."

"On the same farm?"

"Well, we use the same entrance, but my dad and Uncle Frederick subdivided the original farm when my grandfather died, so they could each farm their own way. My dad focused on cattle, and Frederick preferred growing fruit and vegetables. So, Frederick chose the lower side of the farm with more fertile land, leaving us the pastures of the higher side, including this house."

When they had finished eating and the bottle of wine was empty, Joseph cleared the table, and Jen helped him with the dishes. Joseph asked, "Would you like a glass of whiskey or blueberry wine?"

Jen sensed an opportunity to gauge Joseph's intentions for the evening and replied, "Not if I have to drive home." Immediately though, she regretted her words, and made a correction. "I meant to say no thanks, since I'm driving."

"How about coffee then?"

"That would be great."

"I also have dessert that Aunt Annette made."

"Ooh, what is it?"

"I'm not sure, I didn't have time to look under the foil yet."

Jen and Joseph had coffee and rhubarb pie on the front porch as they watched the sun set beyond the rolling pastures of Eldringhoff Farm. Jen didn't want to leave, but she knew she should. So, she stood and told Joseph, "Thanks so much for tonight, but I think it's time for me to go."

Joseph nodded in agreement, then stood as well. Jen approached him. She stood on her toes and stretched as high as she could to kiss his lips, but only for a moment. Joseph walked Jen to her minivan, held the door for her, and said, "Be careful, the deer will be out this time of night."

It wasn't late when Jen returned to Steiner Farm, but she left the boys at the Big House anyway. She dressed for bed and then curled up on the couch, both relieved and disappointed to be sleeping alone.

LI.

With his nephew Bo among the candidates, Fr. Beck was proud to assist the Bishop with the sacrament of Confirmation at St. Hubertus in the spring of 2011. Fr. Beck, though mostly consumed with his official duties, did notice three newcomers to the Steiner family pew, Joseph Eldringhoff and his two daughters. Afterward, Fr. Beck joined the family at the Big House to celebrate.

Fr. Beck greeted Grandma Steiner first, considering it a priority. "Congratulations Grandma, a great-grandson confirmed."

Grandma, in return, addressed Fr. Beck by his earned title. "Thank you for being here, Father."

"Of course."

"You know, as a mother, I didn't appreciate these occasions like I should have. I had so many kids, and I had them so fast that we were covered up with milestones. There were baptisms, birthdays, first communions, graduations, weddings and even an ordination. I'm sorry to say so, but it was a burden having to cook and clean, and get people ready for these things. As a grandma though, I planned to enjoy them, but I was jilted. After Helen passed, I was never invited to celebrate anything with her kids. And Veronica, you know, she married the Baptist, and they don't do sacraments like we do. I went to some graduations for her kids, but that's all. So, with the new generation, Jen's boys, I'll celebrate at every opportunity, at least while I'm still able."

Fr. Beck grabbed a decanter of whiskey from the nearby buffet and filled two glasses. He handed one to Grandma. She raised it and drank the contents in one swig. Fr. Beck did likewise before reiterating, "Congratulations, Grandma."

"Thanks for listening, Father."

Fr. Beck excused himself and mingled until he overheard Joseph talking about the Christmas trees. Joseph was sharing childhood memories of getting Christmas trees from Msgr. Steiner. He said, "Msgr. let us choose and cut our own, and for payment, he suggested a donation in the collection plate the following Sunday. I'm sorry that my girls may not have that same experience." Then, he wondered aloud as to the current condition of the trees.

Fr. Beck interjected, "Many are salvageable, they just need some care."

Fr. Beck took Joseph to the field to inspect the trees. On their way, Joseph dropped some news, "I'd like to marry Jen, but she told me I had to talk to you first."

"Are you asking for my blessing?"
"Yes, I am, Father."
"Do you know why she sent you to me?"

"She's told me about your history together and how much you mean to her."

Fr. Beck tried not to blush, "How much did she tell you?"

Joseph was unflapped. "With what she told me, I can't imagine there could be much she didn't."

"Of course, you'll have my blessing. I would, though, appreciate your candor in answering one more question. Knowing what you know about us, will you have a problem with me being in her life as I am now?"

Joseph didn't hesitate. "Not at all. I trust you both."

LII.

Bo turned thirteen on May 27, 2011. To celebrate, Jen planned to take the boys to the arcade in the Jefferson City mall and invited Fr. Beck to join them.

With the boys distracted by the games, Jen asked Fr. Beck, "Has Joseph talked to you yet about us getting married?"

"We talked about it at the Confirmation."

"Well, what did you tell him?"

"Jen, I've taken a vow of celibacy and he's a great guy, so I gave him the only answer that I could in good faith."

"Well, shit. What the hell is taking him so long then?"

"I don't know, just be patient. I'm sure it'll happen sooner than later."

"I'm living like an anchoress in the meantime though. I'm a young woman still, and it's been a while for me." Jen's voice conveyed her frustration.

Fr. Beck wrinkled his nose and said, "I don't want to hear about your sex life."

Jen had needed to vent, but calmed down and said, "You're the closest thing I have to a girlfriend, so will you please indulge me on this?"

"Alright, fine. How can I indulge you?"

"Go talk to him, and see what you can find out."

"No. You guys have my blessing, but I'm not going to beg him to do it either."

Jen became distracted and didn't respond. Instead, she said, "Stay here with the boys. I'll be right back." She headed to the nearby costume jewelry boutique and approached the lone person in the store, a liberally pierced and tattooed young woman. She asked, "Where's Boone?" Though he had come to see the boys some after his release from prison, his visits had become fewer and farther between until they ceased altogether. Similarly, Boone's child support payments, once only sporadic at best, had ended as well.

"I don't know." The woman was defensive.

Unsure why, Jen was inclined to believe the woman. "He hasn't paid me child support in months."

"Well, at least he paid you ever."

Jen considered the woman's response and muttered, "Shit."

"What?"

Disillusioned, Jen admitted, "I can't believe it, but you've made me feel sorry you. Never mind." Jen returned to the arcade without the boys even noticing that she had left.

Fr. Beck asked, "Who was that?"

"The mother of Boone's other children."

"Have you met her before?"

"Nope."

"How did you know it was her then?"

"I recognized her from Facebook. I wasn't sure it was her when I went over there, but then I saw she had a tattoo of the Queen of Spades on her forearm. Boone always wanted me to get one like that, but I wouldn't let him brand me like a piece of livestock. I didn't keep many boundaries with him, but that was one."

LIII.

The next day, Fr. Beck returned to the mall and found the same woman, again working in the boutique. He waited, pretending to browse while she pierced the ears of a young girl. After the girl and her parents left the store, the woman said to him brusquely, "Like I already told your girlfriend yesterday, I don't know where Boone is."

"That's fine by me because I don't care to ever see him again."

"Oh, so you know him?"

"I'm usually too ashamed of him to admit it, but he's my brother, which means I'm your kids' uncle." Fr. Beck then handed the woman a card with his contact information. "I understand that I'm a stranger to you, but don't be afraid to reach out to me if you or the kids need anything."

Astonished by Fr. Beck's grace, the woman asked, "Are you sure you're Boone's brother?"

LIV.

On the first anniversary of his ordination, Fr. Beck received a phone call from the Bishop's receptionist, Shirley. She first congratulated him and then summoned him to the chancery for a meeting with the Bishop. When Fr. Beck arrived, Shirley showed him to the Bishop's office and shut the door as she left. Skipping pleasantries, the Bishop remarked, "St. Hubertus is a mess."

As a professional courtesy, Fr. Beck resisted the urge to go off on Fr. Bob, so he responded simply, "I know, Bishop."

"Eight kids confirmed, and that was with seventh and eighth grades combined." After a sip of coffee, the bishop stated, "I'm considering closing the parish." Fr. Beck was saddened, but could not dispute the prudence of the Bishop's position, so he remained silent. Continuing, the Bishop noted, "That parish did well under Msgr. Steiner, and I believe they respond better to a priest from their community. So first, I want to see what you can do as pastor."

"I'm honored to have the opportunity." While Fr. Beck's reply was truthful, he felt that he owed the Bishop additional candor. He cleared his throat, then added, "But you should know that the woman lives there." The Bishop didn't respond, instead he just looked at Fr. Beck who then understood that the Bishop's hesitation regarded the seal of confession. "I think it's best if we're be able to discuss this openly, so I'll tell you now, outside of confession, that I have a complicated history with a woman who lives in St. Hubertus."

The Bishop then broke his silence and asked, "Should I be worried about that?" While Fr. Beck considered the question, the Bishop added, "Because I'd rather lose a parish than a priest."

"No." Fr. Beck was clear. "You shouldn't worry."

"Then you'll have one year to show me real progress or I'll have to begin the process of closing St. Hubertus."

LV.

Fr. Beck did not expect to have such a hard time moving into the St. Hubertus rectory. But the small stone bungalow still smelled like Msgr. Steiner and every crossing of the threshold evoked memories, some pleasant, and some not. By mid-afternoon, the rectory was in state of disarray with Fr. Beck's unpacked belongings cluttering the rooms. Fr. Beck, more exhausted emotionally than physically, took a break from unpacking. He found a jar of Msgr.'s homemade whiskey in a kitchen cabinet and poured a glass. He sat down on Msgr.'s recliner, and before he could even take a drink, had to get back up to respond to a knock on the door. He was not surprised to have a visitor, assuming it was just another parishioner welcoming him with food, but he did not expect it to be Sister Paul Joseph. She asked if he could spare a couple minutes for her, and he invited her to sit with him at the kitchen table.

Gesturing at the jar of whiskey, Sister Paul Joseph said, "I have something to tell you and something to ask you, but if you don't mind, I'll have a glass of that first." Fr. Beck poured her a shot, and she took a swig, not quite emptying the glass. "The upcoming school year will be my last as principal. It's too much for me anymore." Fr. Beck did not anticipate such a momentous first day as pastor, but he had prepared himself for tough times. Sister Paul Joseph then admitted, "My mind seems to come and go. I held out as long as I could, praying that I would outlast Fr. Bob because I didn't want him to choose the next principal."

"I understand. I'll work with you to find a suitable replacement."

"Thank you, Father." She seemed to lighten a little with relief. "Now for my question, will you be willing to serve as the trustee for Steiner Farm? I'm afraid I'm not fit to continue in that capacity either."

"Of course." Unprepared for her request and without any understanding of the responsibilities of the trustee, Father Beck accepted the position, certain he would do almost anything to help the Steiner family, if asked. "Can you tell me a little more about being the trustee?"

"I'll need another glass of whiskey first." Fr. Beck poured another glass, and Sister Paul Joseph took a sip this time. "When my father, Gerhard II, died, my mother was lost. She knew nothing about running a farm, so she put it into a trust. She would've preferred for Augustine to act as the trustee, but she didn't want to burden him, since he 'was so busy being a priest.'" It took Father Beck a moment to realize she was referring to Msgr. Steiner. "So, she made me the trustee. She told me to the use the farm to help the family, but it was up to me how I interpreted that." Sister Paul Joseph paused to sip her whiskey again, then continued. "We made some money each year from Pius leasing the farmland. From time to time, I would use some of it for an improvement at the school or a large repair at the church. I even borrowed money against the land if I felt that it was in the family's best interest. We supported Jen with it too, and others who needed help." She raised her glass again, her hand shaking a little. "Things were fine until the school needed a major influx of funds just to pay the teachers. I borrowed what I could, but the bank cut me off. I don't even get enough from the lease to pay the taxes and interest on the loan now." In despair now, Sister Paul Joseph paused for a moment. "If you're still willing to help us, you'll probably have to sell the farm."

Fr. Beck asked, "How bad is it?"

"I owe over $900,000."

Fr. Beck took a drink of whiskey. "What's the farm worth?"

"It's around $3,000 an acre. So, maybe a million, but with the big house, maybe a little more."

Fr. Beck considered how Sister Paul Joseph had sacrificed everything, even her family farm, for the sake others, just as a mother would for her children. "Sister, I don't know what to say." Fr. Beck excused himself for a moment. He went to a stack of boxes in the bedroom, shuffling them until he found his manutergium. He came back to the kitchen and sat in front of Sister Paul Joseph. He handed her the cloth, "I want you to have this."

Sister Paul Joseph took the cloth with careful fingers. She said nothing but the tears in her eyes conveyed plenty.

LVI.

Jimmy and Lillian had lived in the same neighborhood since they were married, first in a one-bedroom apartment, and later, in a three-bedroom house. Now, with four kids and another on the way, Jimmy and Lillian agreed they should find a bigger place to live. They were honest with their realtor about their budget, and she started with homes at the top of it. They weren't just large, but beautiful, and in the nicest neighborhoods. They saw four houses on the first day, and the realtor left them alone in the last, so they could discuss it in private.

Jimmy observed, "This kitchen is larger than our first apartment and my mom's flat combined."

"You should be proud of what you've achieved."

"What did I achieve other than a pile of cash? I hate the money, I hate how we made it, and now I'm going to hate how we spend it."

"Give it all way then, Jim."

Jimmy didn't respond, but looked at Lillian as if to gauge her sincerity. He had stopped drinking, but without alcohol, was still captive to his emotions at times. He was now careful to shield the children from his moods, but Lillian suspected that it was untenable for him to simply mask his struggles forever.

Lillian noticed Jimmy's look and confirmed, "I'm serious. I'd rather stay in our house and go back to teaching, if that would help you find a deep and enduring peace."

Jimmy looked around the cavernous kitchen, then said, "That's not the answer right now. Pick the house you want, and I'll be happy with it."

LVII.

The new house meant a new parish and school. Their third child, Benedict, was about to start kindergarten, and he was invited to a swim party along with all the other kids that would be in his class at St. Elizabeth of Hungary School. The entire family was invited, and although Jimmy groused about it, he went too.

The Wards now lived in a large and opulent home, but it was dwarfed, both in size and luxury, by the estate they visited for the party. The hosts of the party greeted the Wards at the door. A woman with a toddler in her arms and glowing with pregnancy made introductions, "I'm Mary Beth Curry, and these are my parents, Jack and Theresa Hogan. It's actually their house, but they are letting us take it over for the day."

Lillian responded, "We're the Wards. I'm Lillian and this is my husband Jimmy."

From the gaggle of children behind Lillian, Mary Beth picked one and said, "I'll bet you're Benedict."

Benedict was too shy to answer, so Lillian affirmed for him.

Mary Beth then told Benedict, "My daughter, Monica, will be in your class. Would you like to meet her?"

Benedict had warmed a little, and nodded.

Mary Beth then showed her guests to the pool and on the way, chatted with Lillian, while her father Jack asked, "Are you Jimmy Ward of Well-Regulated-Militia fame?"

Embarrassed now, Jimmy nodded in acknowledgment.

"I miss your work. You were a powerful voice for freedom. Come with me, we can talk guns."

Jimmy followed Jack to a set of stairs going down, but noted, "I'm not actually a gun guy. I've never even touched one."

Jack stopped for a moment and looked at Jimmy. "Really?"

"Yeah, I just had a client who I thought had been wronged, so I tried to help him."

"It must be nice to have a passion for your work. I'm in acrylics, and no one is passionate about acrylics." Jack led Jimmy down the flight of stairs.

In the basement now, Jimmy said, "When we were struggling, and I was helping a guy out, I had passion for it, but that changed when I realized that I was making money off the hardships of others."

"So, you have a conscience?"

Jack grabbed two glasses and a decanter of brown liquor, but before he poured the second, Jimmy stopped him, "No thanks. I don't drink anymore."

Jack put the second glass back on the shelf and said, "There's no moral way to make a lot of money." Jimmy thought about Jack's words as he continued, "I've done well, but everything I have belongs to God. I'm just the caretaker of it all during my short time here on earth. God gave it all to me and he can take it all from me, just like my last breath and my next breath."

"Do you have guilt about it?"

"That's why I drink." They laughed and then Jack acknowledged, "My wife and I are human, and some of our spending is sinful. We know that, but we try to be good stewards of the money, using it to support our parish and other good causes. Beyond that, we used our financial security to plant seeds for the future of the Church."

"What do you mean by that?"

"Children. God blessed us seven times, and we were able to focus on raising them to be faithful Catholics as adults. Some already are, and others we're still praying for."

Jimmy and Jack visited a bit longer before joining the rest of the party poolside. Jimmy watched for a moment as Lillian supervised their children and socialized with the other parents. To him, she was starting to look pregnant, but no one else would even suspect it yet. And Jimmy had a new sense of pride in his growing family. It felt like something important and holy that he and Lillian were doing together.

LVIII.

The second time that Jen had dinner at Joseph's house she left Bo in charge of his younger brothers, and before she left said, "I won't be late." Joseph grilled steaks again. Jen was not disappointed, but wondered if the wives of cattlemen ever ate anything else. She smiled at the brand again finding the practice quirky, but charming. Then, she noticed that it wasn't the same symbol as the last time. This one resembled two-thirds of a treble hook.

Joseph asked, "Do you know what that is?"

"No, I can't even guess."

Then, to give Jen a hint, Joseph pointed to the wall above the mantle, where a large piece of iron forged into the same symbol now hung.

Jen looked at it, and after she thought about it, figured out what it was. "It's two J's with their backs to one another." She paused again, then concluded, "It's our brand." Jen got up from her seat at the table and walked over to Joseph. He stood too, and she put her arms as far around him as she could. She pressed her left cheek against his chest and said, "I love you."

Then Joseph asked, "Jen?" She didn't react right away, too comfortable in their embrace, so Joseph repeated, "Jen?"

She sighed in relief, looked up at him, and said, "Don't. This is perfect. The answer is yes."

LIX.

Like most nights during the baseball season, Fr. Beck had fallen asleep in the recliner watching the Cardinals game. He awoke to a knock on the door and in his daze, thought it was the middle of the night. When he opened the door though, it was still light outside, but fading quickly. Jen had Joseph with her, and Fr. Beck assumed why they were there. But he felt better about it than he had anticipated, seeing how unburdened she looked.

When Jen confirmed the reason for their visit, Fr. Beck said, "Congratulations to you both," and he welcomed them inside.

Jen wasn't even through the door before she asked, "How soon can we do this."

Fr. Beck answered, "Diocesan policy is six months."

"I was hoping to do it sooner, like tonight, if possible."

Fr. Beck laughed, but Jen looked like she wanted an answer, so he replied, "I'll talk to the Bishop to see about an exception, but you're not getting married tonight."

"What's the point of having a priest as a friend if you can't just get married on a whim?"

Fr. Beck smiled and asked, "How about a celebratory drink?" Fr. Beck went to the kitchen and poured three glasses of whiskey. As he handed the first to Jen, he noticed her ring. The last time he had seen her wearing a ring was the day she had told him she was pregnant and marrying his brother. The woman standing before him now was preparing for a sacramental marriage to a righteous man, but the girl that day fourteen years ago, was not. Fr. Beck dropped the glass. It didn't break, but bounced when it hit the tile floor, spilling the whiskey. He closed his eyes, but was overwhelmed by a spinning sensation. He tried to catch himself on the counter, but missed it and collapsed to the floor.

When he woke up, he was sitting on the kitchen floor, leaning against the cabinets for support. Jen was kneeling beside him, shaking him and repeating his name.

Finally, he was able to answer. "What?"

"What happened? Are you okay?"

Fr. Beck thought about it, but couldn't remember at first, then answered in a meek voice, "You were just a girl."

Jen then sat next to him and replied, "So what?"

"And you were so vulnerable then. I said I loved you, but I left you here with him." Fr. Beck sighed. "I knew who he was and what he would do to you, and I let it happen."

"Cole, I thought we were beyond this a long time ago." Jen's tone was as sweet as he had ever heard it.

"I made peace with you, but I've never forgiven myself." Cole shook his head in shame. "It's my worst sin and I've never confessed it."

She stood and grabbed his arm to help him up. Then, she looked him in the eyes and said, "I'm going to be okay now."

She escorted him to the recliner and went to the kitchen to get some ice for his head.

Looking around, Cole asked, "Where's Joseph?"

"He went to get Dr. Isringhausen."

"He's a veterinarian."

Jen shrugged.

When Dr. Isringhausen arrived, he asked Fr. Beck to describe what happened and gave him a cursory exam. Then, he asked Jen, "Have you been keeping up with his heartworm medication?" No one laughed, so Dr. Isringhausen apologized, and said "I had something similar happen to me when I came back from Vietnam. I was driving through the bootheel on my way to New Orleans for Mardis Gras. I saw a rice paddy, had a spell, and drove my car off in the ditch. War is traumatic. And with your history, something like this can be expected."

Fr. Beck lied, "You're right. It was probably something like that."

Jen made eye contact with Cole and smiled through the otherwise pained look on her face.

LX.

During Lillian's first four pregnancies, Jimmy had missed more prenatal appointments than he made, but this time, he was doting. Lillian found the visits superfluous, with the twenty-week ultrasound as the exception, as it revealed many indicators as to the health and development of the baby. On their way to the ultrasound, Lillian admitted, "I'm nervous. Thanks for coming."

Jimmy regretted that he had set the bar so low that his wife felt the need to show appreciation for something this basic. He wanted to apologize, but it wasn't the time to start a conversation that may be upsetting, so he went with the safest response. "You're welcome."

While they waited to see the doctor after the ultrasound, Lillian said to Jimmy, "Something's wrong."

Jimmy tried to be supportive. "I'm sure everything's fine."

Lillian was adamant though. "The technician usually talks my ear off, but this time, she hardly said anything."

"Maybe because I was there."

"No Jim, something's wrong."

When the doctor came into the exam room, he confirmed Lillian's suspicion, explaining "There are abnormalities with the baby's heart, lungs, and kidneys. She can survive the pregnancy, but…"

Lillian cried on their ride home, and when they arrived, she gathered herself before entering the house to not alarm the children. But when she walked through the door, the children leapt on her, peppering their mother with questions about the baby. Jimmy tried to redirect them, but Lillian waved him and gathered them around her, "Come look at pictures of your sister." Then, she took a deep breath and looked at each of the children in turn. "I have something important to tell you. Your sister's name will be Margaret, for Blessed Margaret of Castello. We can call her Maggie though." Lillian stopped, as though she would say no more, but then said, "God decided that she is not going to live with us, but in heaven with Him. We'll miss her, but we're happy that God would think so much of her that He decided to keep her with Him."

Jimmy watched his wife with astonishment as Lillian fielded dozens of questions, both medical and theological, from the children with composure and grace. She gave truthful, yet age appropriate responses. Lillian continued until the children were pacified. Then, she turned to Jimmy and announced, "I need to leave for a while."

Jimmy said, "Okay," but Lillian was already gone.

Hours past and Lillian hadn't returned, so Jimmy fed and bathed the children, then put them to bed. He wanted to call her to see if she was okay, but decide to let her have peace and time alone. So, he waited patiently, but in the stillness, could no longer avoid processing the news. He was devastated, but at the same time, never felt less sorry for himself.

Lillian returned near midnight, and Jimmy asked her where she had gone.

"Church." Jimmy looked at the clock, so Lillian added, "The adoration chapel is always open."

"Are you okay?"

"I'm exhausted."

"You were courageous today." Jimmy wondered whether that was attributable to his failures. "Where did you find the strength?"

"Faith that God won't give me more than I can handle."

"I just don't have that type of relationship with God."

"That's because you're too worried about what the world wants you to do and what people think of you. I try my best to do God's will and only concern myself with what He thinks of me. And He's entrusted me to bear this cross, so I will."

The next morning, Jimmy asked Lillian, "I need to address some unfinished business in St. Hubertus. Will you be okay without me today?"

Lillian laughed. "I think we can manage without you for a day."

LXI.

The man who answered the rectory door was not who Jimmy expected. He was much younger and not even dressed like a priest. "I'm sorry to bother you, but my name's Jimmy Ward, and I'm looking for the priest."

"I'm Father Beck."

"Beck? Are you related to Boone?"

"Unfortunately, yes." Fr. Beck asked, "Is that why you're here?"

"No, actually, I was looking for a different priest."

"One in particular?"

"Yes, the last time I saw him, he was pruning Christmas trees in a cassock."

"That would be Msgr. Steiner, but he's no longer with us."

"Different parish?"

"No, sadly, he died. Is there something I can help you with?"

Jimmy thought about it, then replied, "I hope so."

Father Beck held the door open, welcoming Jimmy inside the rectory. Fr. Beck offered his guest coffee and a seat at the kitchen table. He poured two cups from a pot that was already made, and asked, "How can I help you?"

"Msgr. told me I could come here and confess my sins when I was ready." Fr. Beck nodded in encouragement. "But it's been so long I'm not even sure how to do it or where to start."

Fr. Beck set the coffee cups on the kitchen table and grabbed his stole from the living room. He suggested, "Why don't you just start with what's bothering you the most?"

Jimmy looked at the ceiling and then back at Fr. Beck. He took a deep breath and said, "I took advantage of my wife. I neglected her, burdened her, and cheated on her. I was emotionally unavailable to my children. I dishonored my mother. I profited from the loss of human life…." Jimmy continued to list his sins and Fr. Beck let him speak without interruption. Then, when Jimmy stopped, Fr. Beck asked, "Are you sorry for these sins?"

Jimmy answered, "I am."

"And for any sins you haven't mentioned?"

"I'm sorry for those as well."

Fr. Beck asked, "Will you do your penance, which is to pray a rosary for your children?"

"I will."

"And finally, are you committed to amending your life?"

"Yes, Father."

After Fr. Beck said the prayer of absolution, Jimmy thanked him and took a sip of coffee before asking, "May I trouble you about something else?"

"Certainly."

"My wife and I got some unfortunate news yesterday." Jimmy's voice became shaky. "The baby we're expecting, she should be fine while she's in there, but she can't live out here."

Fr. Beck was quiet for a moment and then said, "I'm so sorry to hear that."

Jimmy then looked Fr. Beck in the eyes and asked, "Is this my punishment?"

Fr. Beck shook his head and said, "No."

Walking to his SUV in the church parking lot, Jimmy saw a doe and her fawn in the November twilight. He watched as they leaped the fence into Steiner Farm and melted into the Christmas trees. Then, Jimmy noticed the "For Sale" sign at the entrance to the farm. He looked at the modest farmhouse in the distance, then took down the realtor's number.

It was late when Jimmy returned home, and the children were already in bed. He found Lillian in the family room, sitting with her rosary in hand. He didn't want to disturb her prayer, so he started to leave the room, but she asked, "How was your day?"

Jimmy thought for a moment before answering, "Sanctifying."

"Sanctifying? How so?"

"I had a conversation with a priest, and went to confession for the first time in a long time, and now I'm ready to make some changes."

"I'm glad to hear that."

"I know it's a bad time now, with yesterday's news, but I'd like for us to have a fresh start, somewhere else, after the baby…" Jimmy couldn't say it, so he changed direction mid-sentence. "…After things settle down for us."

Lillian looked at Jimmy and said, "We just moved here."

Jimmy understood her objection. "I know, and I'm also aware that I said I would like the house that you picked, but this isn't God's will for us."

Lillian surprised Jimmy. "I agree. I thought I would like it here, but this house isn't right for us."

Jimmy explained, "I don't just want a new house, but to make a new life, where we are close to nature, doing yeoman's work together as a family."

"Like a homestead?"

"No, a Christmas tree farm in St. Hubertus."

"We're city people, Jim, not farmers, and you hate Christmas."

"You're right, but like I said, I'm ready to make some changes."

Lillian thought for a moment, then said, "I appreciate your enthusiasm for starting a new life together, but I'm not going to move my kids to a town I've never visited and into a house I've never seen."

"That's fine. The realtor's going to meet us there at noon on Saturday."

LXII.

Jimmy and Lillian toured the Big House and the rest of Steiner Farm on Saturday afternoon. Afterward, they stopped for dinner at Frau's Haus. Lillian was quiet while she ate, but when finished, she said, "I feel like this is the right thing to do, but the house is just too small for our family."

"I understand." Jimmy was disappointed.

Lillian explained, "I just don't see how the Steiners raised thirteen kids there. But if you're willing to put an addition on the house, I'm ready to move here."

"So, after we have some closure with Maggie?" Jimmy hated to bring it up, but wanted to understand his wife's intentions.

"No, as soon as possible. If this is going to be our home, I want her buried at St. Hubertus."

After dinner, Jimmy and Lillian drove the thirty miles from St. Hubertus to the Lake of the Ozarks. Jimmy had hoped to stay at the Osage View Motor Inn, the quaint roadside motel where they had spent their honeymoon. But when they arrived, Jimmy and Lillian agreed that either they or the Osage View had changed, or both. So, they kept driving and stopped for the night at one of the Lake's new and luxurious resorts.

Jimmy and Lillian hadn't slept in the same bed for years. When Jimmy was struggling, the intimacy of sleeping in a bed with his wife was more than he could bear, and at some point, it had become a habit that he didn't know how to break. So, he roamed the house each night, sleeping for short spells in a chair or on a couch. That night though, they shared one room with one bed. Jimmy was almost as nervous getting into to bed with his wife that night as he was the first time he did so, at the Osage View, nearly fifteen years prior. But his anxiety melted away when Lillian took his hand and placed it on her stomach, and together, they felt Maggie frolic.

On their way back to St. Louis in the morning, Jimmy and Lillian stopped at St. Hubertus for Sunday mass. In lieu of a traditional homily, Fr. Beck gave what he called a "state of the parish address." He announced that "the parish and school faced closure" and explained that he needed "people in the pews, students in the school, and money in the coffers," to keep them open. To meet this goal, Fr. Beck offered to "waive tuition for any families who attended mass, made an honest effort to tithe, and volunteered at one fundraising event per year."

When they returned to their SUV after mass, Lillian noted, "The situation sounds pretty bleak here. Maybe we should reconsider."

Jimmy thought for a moment, then said, "You're right, it does sound bleak, but now I'm even more sure that we should do this."

LXIII.

With the farm under contract to Jimmy and Lillian Ward in December of 2011, Grandma Steiner moved to a nursing home at ninety-seven years old. She had lived in the Big House for seventy-five years, but on the property even longer. Her first three children were born in the old cabin, the next nine in the Big House, and the last, Paula, in a barn. Departing her longtime home for the final time, Grandma thought about the family she had raised there.

Grandma couldn't understand how she had ended up with fewer grandchildren than children. At times, she tried to rationalize it, citing two children in religious life and another who died too young, but most of the time, she just found it tragic. Even excusing Josephine as barren, that still left nine kids to have just eight grandkids. All her grandchildren were from daughters, and she lamented, "after Heinrich, there will be no more Steiners of St. Hubertus." Then she thought about Gerhard, and whether the rumor about him was true, having a child out of wedlock. Though it would have created quite the scandal at the time, in retrospect, she now wished that it was.

It was not just the lack of grandchildren that tormented her though, but that some of her children cared so little about the reputation and legacy of the Steiner family. Grandma was proud of Jen though. With all her faults and struggles along the way, she persevered and finally had her life together. Grandma delighted in her great grandsons, calling them Steiners, fully aware they were actually Becks. And while Grandma was bitter to be moving to a nursing home, she took a cold comfort knowing that Steiner Farm would not be a windfall for her wayward children. To Grandma, Steiner Farm had already helped people who deserved it, and her children could fend for themselves.

LXIV.

When Father Beck went to the title agent's office to finalize the sale of the farm, he was surprised to see it was Jimmy who had bought it, and was delighted to meet Lillian. Nearing her due date, her body was stressed from pregnancy, but Father Beck knew about the situation and didn't risk congratulating her. He did though, invite his new neighbors to dinner at Frau's Haus afterward.

The title agent interrupted, handing a check to Fr. Beck, made out to the Steiner Farm Trust for just under $30,000, the amount left after the debt, taxes, and fees were satisfied. He had intended to use the money to help Jen find interim housing between the farm sale and her upcoming wedding, but Joseph already took care of that, renting her a house in town. Fr. Beck thought about offering to reimburse Joseph, but instead chose to let him take care of his future wife.

At Frau's Haus, Lillian discussed the expected loss of their daughter, Maggie. Father Beck found some consoling words, but felt that Lillian was at peace already. Father Beck even offered to come to the hospital for the birth, so he could baptize Maggie, but Jimmy interjected, "Thanks, but we'll still be in St. Louis."

Undeterred, Father Beck insisted, "I can be there, if you'll have me."

Lillian spoke up and settled the matter. "I'd feel even better with you in the delivery room."

Their food arrived, and while they ate, Jimmy said, "Father, we heard your 'state of the parish' homily, and Lillian and I would like to help."

"We'll take whatever help we can get."

Then Lillian said, "If you haven't already filled the principal position, I'd like to be considered for the job."

"That's great, I'll be happy to introduce you to Sister Paul Joseph, she's helping me interview candidates."

Lillian then added, "If I get the job, I won't require a salary."

Surprised, Father Beck responded, "Are you sure?"

"We have four children at or near school age and I'm about to bury my baby here." Lillian's voiced cracked and she took a moment before finishing in a calm and clear tone. "It's imperative that the parish and school remain open. We need them for our family."

After some silence, Jimmy said, "I also think we can use the farm to help the church."

Fr. Beck asked, "How so?"

Jimmy explained, "I don't know anything about farming and even less about farming Christmas trees. So, I already planned to hire help, and don't expect to be left with much, if any, profit. But instead of hiring workers, maybe we could get volunteers from the parish to work at the farm. Then, we can sell the trees each season and the parish can keep the proceeds."

Fr. Beck liked the idea, but wasn't even sure if he answered before being distracted by a server pushing two tables together for a large party. It was Jen with her boys and Joseph with his girls. While Bo helped seat the younger kids, Joseph and Jen came over to say hello. Fr. Beck made formal introductions, but acknowledged "I believe Jen and Jimmy and are already acquainted."

Jen responded, "Yeah, the three of us survived Boone. We should have weekly meetings, but I'm not sure there's enough liquor in town to talk about it."

Boone was an unpleasant topic for the group, so Fr. Beck changed the subject filling Jen and Joseph in on Jimmy's proposal. "If we open the Christmas tree farm as a fundraiser for the parish, how much do you think it could make?"

Joseph considered the question and said, "There's about forty acres of trees. So, forty to fifty thousand dollars each year. Maybe even sixty, if the trees are in good condition."

Jimmy asked, "What about the rest of the farmland? There's another hundred and twenty or so arable acres. We could plant trees there too, right?"

Joseph responded, "Sure. It would take several years for the trees to be big enough to sell though."

"So, eventually we could make a quarter million each year?" Fr. Beck was blown away by the potential.

Joseph concurred, "I don't see why not."

Jen suggested, "We could use the old cabin like a country store. When people come to buy the trees, parishioners could sell baked or canned goods, or quilts, even Christmas crafts."

They became so excited by the prospect that they were talking over each other with a rush of ideas. Less than two weeks later, Fr. Beck held a meeting to brief the entire parish on the proposal and to ask for a commitment from volunteers.

LXV.

When Lillian met with Fr. Beck and Sister Paul Joseph to interview for the position of principal of the St. Hubertus School, she was nearing the end of her pregnancy. Fr. Beck made sure that Sister Paul Joseph was aware of the situation before their meeting. He didn't though inform Sister Paul Joseph about Lillian's offer to work for free, believing that the best fit may not be the least expensive candidate.

Early in the interview, Sister Paul Joseph noted that with Fr. Beck waiving tuition for active parishioners, she expected "enrollment to increase by as much as fifty percent for the next school year."

Lillian then asked, "Is there a plan to hire additional staff?"

Fr. Beck sighed. "The financial position of the parish is already untenable. I'm looking forward to a boon after Thanksgiving, with the Christmas tree farm set to open, so maybe we can do it then."

Lillian looked concerned, but answered, "I understand, Father."

The woman before him was not just an interviewee, but a new parishioner who had taken a chance on his parish. Fr. Beck sensed her disillusionment and felt he needed to explain. "I've already asked the parishioners for money and fundraising volunteers, and they've responded, but it's just not enough."

Then, Lillian asked with grace, "But have you asked for their prayers, Father?"

Father Beck was embarrassed to admit, "No, not explicitly." He turned to Sister Paul Joseph and said, "But Msgr. would have."

After the interview, Fr. Beck walked Lillian out. When he returned, Sister Paul Joseph was packing her notepad in her canvas tote. She said, "Cancel the rest of the interviews. She's the one."

Fr. Beck was moved by Lillian's suggestion, and he once again challenged the parish, this time in a letter.

My Brothers and Sisters in Christ,

For over forty years, the Blessed Sacrament was exposed at St. Hubertus in perpetual adoration. During that period, the parish thrived. With the practice suspended, we struggle. Effective immediately, Eucharistic adoration will return to St. Hubertus. It will not be perpetual at first, but with your commitment, it could be soon. Please also pray for your Pastor, that the Holy Spirit guides him as he shepherds the parish through this difficult time, and always remember, the Eucharist is all that matters.

In Christ, Fr.

Fr. Beck led by example, covering the hour before and the hour after 7:00am mass, Monday through Saturday, just as Msgr. Steiner had done. Former adorers, who had abandoned the practice during the Fr. Bob regime returned. Newcomers also signed up, excited to see their name on the adoration schedule, which was posted on the church bulletin board. And after just a few weeks, the church remained occupied and unlocked at all hours of the day and night.

LXVI.

Per St. Hubertus tradition, the groom and groomsmen met at the rectory for several cocktails with the priest prior to going to church for the wedding. The definition of "several" varied, depending on the families involved and the circumstances of the wedding. In this case, Fr. Beck and Joseph were the only ones old enough to drink.

Msgr. Steiner's cache of liquor was running low, so Fr. Beck was glad to receive a jug of Eldringhoff whiskey from Joseph as a gift for officiating the wedding. Fr. Beck reciprocated, handing a gift to Joseph. It was his first confessional stole. Fr. Beck explained, "A priest is supposed to give this to his father at his first mass. The priest's father is then buried with the stole to present when raised on the last day. I did not have a father at my first mass, so I saved it, but I want you to have it now."

Joseph asked, "But why me?"

"Children first learn about justice and mercy from their father. Let this stole be a reminder of the duty that you have to your daughters, that you now have to my nephews, and that you will have with any future children."

Joseph thanked him, and Fr. Beck did not want to dwell on it, so he changed the subject. Both men took one more drink of whiskey, gathered the four groomsmen, and left for the church.

By modern standards, the reception was small and casual, with about fifty people gathering at the parish hall for cake and punch. Though busy greeting guests, Jen found a moment to speak with Fr. Beck. As she approached him, Fr. Beck greeted her, "Mrs. Eldringhoff."

Jen smiled and quipped, "It just kind of rolls off the tongue, doesn't it?" Fr. Beck laughed, then Jen said, "That was really sweet what you did. It means a lot to Joseph, and even more to me."

Fr. Beck nodded, then excused himself to bless the food, so the cake could be cut.

LXVII.

Two weeks later, Jimmy called Father Beck in the middle of the night to let him know they were going to the hospital. Father Beck left within minutes and drove to St. Louis. When he arrived, he took a seat in the corner of the delivery room. While Lillian labored, Father Beck prayed that the baby would not suffer and that the parents would be healed.

When Maggie was born, the doctor set her on Lillian's chest, and she cradled her baby. Jimmy sat next to his wife on the bed and put a hand on his daughter's back. Father Beck kept his distance, but when Lillian looked to him, he stood, approached the bed, and baptized and confirmed Margaret Castello Ward before she passed.

On the morning of Maggie's funeral, the rain came in waves and the wind seemed to blow from all directions. During the mass, the rain turned to snow and the wind, now steady, howled only from the north. It swept across Steiner Farm, whistled through the Christmas trees, and smacked the mourners in the face as they processed to the cemetery.

The big and wet flakes common to March snows accumulated on Fr. Beck's shoulders and biretta before he had even reached the iron gate at the cemetery entrance. Through the gate, the solemn march continued toward a new and imposing monument in a previously vacant section of the graveyard. The mighty stone was capped by a statue of St. Michael and was engraved with the name Ward.

Fr. Beck passed a row of Steiner graves first. Then there were Eldringhoffs, Stecks, Schneiders, and Isringhausens. There were more rows with more names, but Fr. Beck became distracted as he neared the area where he had first encountered the "man in the black dress" almost two decades ago, now clad in a cassock of his own.

At the gravesite, Fr. Beck removed his biretta and handed it to Bo, who was serving the funeral along with his brothers. Fr. Beck sprinkled the tiny casket with holy water and incensed it as part of the Final Commendation. And when the Rite of Committal was complete, Fr. Beck dismissed his shivering nephews as the mourners dispersed.

Fr. Beck remained at the gravesite with Jimmy, Lillian, and their children. The children were cold and wet and began to fuss. Lillian just ignored them as she stared past the casket and into the hole in the ground. Jimmy said, "I don't think mommy's ready to leave yet, but I'll take you guys to the Big House to get dry clothes and something to eat." Their four-year old, Mary Regina, did not want to leave her mother, but Jimmy took her anyway. She fought him and slipped away as they neared the iron gate.

Mary Regina ran toward Lillian, but lost her footing in the snow and fell hard. Now covered in mud and snow, she cried, "Mommy?" Lillian turned and ran to her daughter without hesitation. She scooped her up and calmed her. Lillian then carried Mary Regina back to the iron gate, and departed St. Hubertus cemetery with her husband and all but one of their children.

Epilogue

Entering his meeting with the Bishop, Fr. Beck was nervous, but resolved to let God's will be done, so he sat in silence while the Bishop read the report. Still looking at the paper, the Bishop observed, "I see here that mass attendance is up, as is school enrollment and collections.

"That's correct Bishop."

"But you also mentioned a, let's see here, a substantial budget deficit."

"Yes, Bishop."

"And you increased expenditures?"

"Yes."

"Why would you increase spending when you couldn't pay the bills you already had?"

Fr. Beck's voiced raised a bit, "I had to do something."

The Bishop snapped back, "Don't get defensive, I'm just trying to understand your theory here."

"The theory is evangelization. The school is the best lure we have. People want their kids in a Catholic school, but can't or won't spend the money on it. We take the kids, catechize them and they bring the faith home. It's like a tree. The roots absorb water and nutrients and deliver sustenance to its limbs. The children will ask their parents, 'Why don't we pray before meals' and 'Why aren't we going to church on Sunday.' Off guard, some of the parents will give in out of shame. The others, even if they aren't interested in church going, will show up to support their children. So, we give the kids roles in the mass; readings, petitions, singing performances, or whatever. The parents will come to watch their kids. They may even like what they hear me say, or they will be overwhelmed by our charity. Hopefully and eventually, they will want to be a part of the community."

After hearing enough the Bishop responded, "How much is it? The shortfall."

"Well, with school enrollment up, we had to…"

The Bishop interrupted, "How much?"

"Almost $100,000."

The Bishop made a pained face and remained silent so long that Fr. Beck thought that it may still be his turn speak. The Bishop finally spoke. "I see." Fr. Beck braced for bad news as the Bishop continued, "Diocese wide, we had a net loss this year in mass attendance and collections. Only in your parish did school and church attendance go up." He looked directly at Father Beck, "What's happening at St. Hubertus is the most exciting thing going on around here and I'm not going to let money stop your work there."

Turning toward the office door, the Bishop barked, "Shirley!?" Instead of using the intercom, the Bishop preferred to just yell through the wall at his receptionist. Shirley appeared almost instantly.

"Yes Bishop?"

"Will you please call Fred at the bank? Tell him a Fr. Beck will come to see him, and that I vouch for St. Hubertus."

"Yes, Bishop."

Relieved, Fr. Beck said, "Thank you" after the office door closed.

"No, thank you, but please understand that there is a limit to this."

"I understand, Bishop."

As Fr. Beck stood to leave, the Bishop asked, "How is . . ." The Bishop struggled to find the right words to describe the situation and ultimately spoke unartfully anyway. "How are things with your woman? With you two living so close."

Fr. Beck responded, "She's not mine anymore." But then, Fr. Beck added, "And I don't think she ever was."

Made in the USA
Coppell, TX
20 February 2020